"I'm still having a hard time believing you're not human." She ran her hand down his arm. He felt as warm as if he'd been in the summer sun for hours. "You feel human." *Really, really human.* Her face grew hot as she stared at him.

He cocked an eyebrow, the look on his face saying he suspected what was going through her mind. "I'm half human. My mother's human. My father's a guardian, like our mutual friend."

She searched his face. "He said you have feelings for me." She stared into the depths of those magical eyes. "Do you?" She could almost feel what he kept protected in his heart. Knowing more about him, she could see the inhuman part of him, the wildness she had sensed, dance in those blue, blue eyes.

He brushed his knuckles over her cheek. "Yes," he admitted. "I do."

She closed her eyes and held his hand to her face. She stepped closer to him. "We can be together, right? I mean, your parents are together."

"Yes. She gave up everything to be with him. She understood how important the guardians are to the fairy world." He leaned down and whispered, "Could you give up everything for me?"

"Right now, yes, I could." Her chest heaved as she tried to catch her breath.

He leaned a little closer, dropping his hand to the side of her neck, then to her collar bone. "But it wouldn't be for just now. It would be forever."

Night Angel

by

Annette Miller

Angel Haven Series

This is a work of fiction. Names, characters, places, and incidents are either the product of the author's imagination or are used fictitiously, and any resemblance to actual persons living or dead, business establishments, events, or locales, is entirely coincidental.

Night Angel

COPYRIGHT © 2014 by Annette Miller

All rights reserved. No part of this book may be used or reproduced in any manner whatsoever without written permission of the author or The Wild Rose Press, Inc. except in the case of brief quotations embodied in critical articles or reviews.
Contact Information: info@thewildrosepress.com

Cover Art by *Angela Anderson*

The Wild Rose Press, Inc.
PO Box 708
Adams Basin, NY 14410-0708
Visit us at www.thewildrosepress.com

Publishing History
First Black Rose Edition, 2014
Print ISBN 978-1-62830-293-6
Digital ISBN 978-1-62830-294-3

Angel Haven Series
Published in the United States of America

Dedication

For my husband Brian and my sons Scot and Alex,
who always believed I could realize my dream

Prologue

July

The High Mother paced in front of the dais, her dress swirling around her ankles. The full moon's light flooded the reception chamber through the tall, narrow windows, adding its cold beam to the warm glow of the candles. Shadows danced over the elder gargoyle's elongated face and the small horns jutting from her forehead, making her charcoal gray, rocky skin appear darker. Her large, dragon-like wings, arcing over her head and almost touching the floor, looked too big for her slim body and were folded tightly against her back. Her silver hair escaped the bun coiled at the nape of her neck.

The long tapestries fluttered as the guardian hurried into the stone chamber, his claws clicking on the polished granite floor. He went to one knee, bowing his head. "You summoned me, High Mother?"

"Yes." She turned as she beckoned him to stand. "Distressing news has reached me from the northeast clan. Caledon's werewolf pack has been attacked."

The guardian frowned as he shook his head, his ebony hair falling into his eyes. "Who would be crazy enough to do that? Even the vampire lords don't mess with Caledon. They learned that lesson at least fifty years ago."

"The attack came, not from the fairy realm, but from humans," she said, her voice barely above a whisper.

The soft light allowed the guardian to see weariness etched into the High Mother's face. He went to her, easing her down in the chair. "More and more humans are displaying extraordinary powers. It would've had to be someone with that kind of ability to take the werewolves. Who was grabbed?"

She laid her hand on his arm. "They took nine children from the pack, including Caledon's first born son and youngest daughter."

"How did they get them?" he asked, his fingers curling into a tight fist.

She rubbed her eyes, then pinched the bridge of her nose. "The school bus was high-jacked."

He stood in front of her, his back rigid. "What about the northeast clan? What have they tried to get the kids back?"

"They followed the kidnappers to a human estate in northern New York." She turned away as tears began to fall. "They never returned."

He squeezed his eyes shut. As gargoyles, he and his brethren were damn near impossible to hurt, let alone kill. "How did they fall?"

"One of the guardians escaped and lived long enough to say the humans have learned of our weakness." She paused. "He didn't last the night."

The guardian held her hand. "You should rest."

She smiled at him and patted his hand. "I will. I called you here because Caledon has requested only the best of all guardians to come to his aid."

He frowned. "Why me? Marshall is the better

fighter. He's bigger and stronger, and he's been a guardian longer than I have."

The High Mother stood. "I know," she said. "But the Oracle insists it must be you who goes. Marshall wouldn't live past two weeks. He's much too..."

The guardian grinned, his long teeth shining in the moonlight. "Hot-headed?"

"I was going to say stubborn and impulsive." She smiled. "I guess hot-headed fits."

He paused. "If the Oracle saw Marshall's death, what will happen to me?"

"The human leader will hurt you. Badly. He's looking for something." She placed her fingers under his chin. "I don't want to send you, but Caledon's request cannot be ignored. To do so would strain relations between the clans."

"Great," he mumbled. "This gets better all the time."

"There is one good thing." She waited as he turned his eyes to hers. "It is there you will meet your soul mate."

His eyes widened, and he inhaled sharply. His soul mate. After decades of wondering if he'd ever find his perfect love, the time was now at hand. "How will I know her?"

She cupped his face. "Look in her eyes. You will see the dragon spirit in her. She will fight for you and by you. She will seek you out."

"When?" he asked. "When will she come?"

"Like all good things, you must wait. She will be there, but not right away." She pulled him close in a tight hug before stepping back, tears shining in her eyes. "Now go and prepare. Safe journey, guardian."

He bowed and left the chamber, striding to his room. He silently mourned his fallen brothers, then crammed his clothes in a small suitcase.

A larger gargoyle pushed the door open and stepped inside. "So, you decided to go?"

He frowned. "I thought the younger brother was supposed to barge into the older brother's room." He nodded. "And yes, Marshall, I'm going."

Marshall grabbed him in a fierce hug. "I heard what's going to happen to you. Be careful, little brother."

He grabbed his brother by the shoulders. "You just stay here. I don't want to lose you."

They stared at each other before Marshall nodded once and left.

He stretched out, waiting for sunrise when he would turn human and make his way to upstate New York. He was anxious to get going. His soul mate was waiting for him. He couldn't help but wonder. What did a woman who carried a dragon spirit look like? And would she accept him after finding out what he was?

Chapter One

October

The opening strains of "Jessie's Girl" by Rick Springfield filled Karen's car. "Oh, shut up." She stabbed the next program button. "Deep breath," she said. "One must remain calm." She sighed. This murder mystery weekend was supposed to relax her. She'd had way too many emotional outbursts lately and needed to regain her focus.

A girl, even a superhero, needed space, and time in the countryside of upstate New York was just what the doctor ordered. Her martial arts skills and rapid healing wasn't giving her body the break it needed from the stress she'd been under lately. She'd insisted she would be fine, was, in fact, fine. Her team, the Angels, just about pushed her out the door. With her recent bad break-up and the villain team, Medusa, making a reappearance, they'd wanted her to get away. She smiled. Their team telepath, Rena, threatened to kick her butt if she didn't go.

Silver gray clouds were rolling in from the west and the wind picked up, bending trees and bouncing her small car around the narrow road. Dirt blew across the two-lane road from the shoulder, and leaf-covered rocky hills rose steeply to either side.

She grabbed the directions off the seat. "Where's

the turn? I don't think I missed it."

Karen slowed down, searching every opening for the gate to the Troyington estate. The dashboard clock clicked another minute closer to the top of the hour, reminding her she was supposed to be there by five. Her left foot tapped against the floor. She took another deep breath and released it. "Calm," she reminded herself. She would arrive when she was supposed to and not before.

Rounding the next bend, she saw a man walking along the edge of the road, his boots stirring up little clouds of dust behind him. His black T-shirt rippled, and his faded blue jeans were tight against his legs as the wind whipped around him. *Where's that guy's jacket? It's the middle of October.* He carried an oversized backpack slung over one shoulder, the material straining at the straps, the bottom sagging. She pulled alongside him, lowering the window with a push of a button.

"Excuse me," she called out. "I think I'm lost. Could you give me directions?"

He paused, then bent down, peering inside. He gazed at her for a moment, his eyes narrowing. "Where're you going?"

Karen stared at him, trembling as every nerve in her body jumped to attention. His square jaw needed a shave, and his skin was tanned too deep for this time of year. His black hair glimmered indigo in the early evening light. But it was his eyes that captured her. Ice blue and untamed, they held a hint of something strange and wild, something magical.

"What?" she stammered, watching his chest rise and fall and the muscles in his arm tighten as he leaned on her car.

"I said, where're you going?" he repeated, his thick, southern drawl making his impatience sound polite.

His rolling accent caressed her body, making her shiver. "The Troyington estate. I think I might've missed the turn."

"No, you haven't missed it." He nodded in the direction she'd been heading. "Just keep going that way for another quarter mile. The turn will be on your right." Pausing, he looked at the sky where clouds had darkened to an ugly gray. When he peered at her again, his eyes seemed to reflect the wild weather. "You'd better get going. The sun's going down soon, and you don't want to be caught out here in the dark when the storm hits." He straightened, adjusted the backpack, and continued on.

Karen watched the easy gait and the roll of his hips as she put the window up. She frowned as disappointment filled her at the thought of never seeing him again. "Get a grip."

As she pulled away, the sky opened up, pelting the windshield with fat raindrops. She flipped the wipers on, looking in the rearview mirror at the black haired man. She knew he had to be soaked through in seconds from the deluge that poured from the sky. She wondered briefly if she should give him a ride. No. That particular storyline had just played out on her favorite soap opera, ending badly for the heroine.

"Finally," she sighed as the drive appeared on her right. Pulling up in front of the mansion, she grabbed her bag and jumped out of the car, running for the covered porch. She pushed her thick brown hair back, trying to shake some of the water from it. As she reached to ring the bell, the door opened. The butler stood there, tall and skeletal, his skin almost as white as his thinning hair.

Behold the walking dead. "Hi, I'm Karen Spraiker."

"Yes, ma'am. We've been expecting you," the butler said, his voice as hollow as his sunken cheeks. He held out a bony hand. "You have your invitation?"

"Yes." She dug around in her purse, pulling out the engraved ivory envelope.

He stepped to the side, and she walked past him into the hall. Warm light filled the entryway, and as she handed him her coat, a tall man stepped out of a room to her left. "Ms. Spraiker, welcome. I'm Bradford Troyington."

His khaki pants were sharply creased, and the light green polo shirt he wore had been pressed to perfection. His blond hair was styled in the most current fashion. As he shook her hand, Karen noted the softness of it. He probably doesn't lift anything heavier than a laptop, she thought. The only tan he'd ever get would be from a salon. Karen thought about the man on the road. He and Bradford were as different as night and day.

Bradford pulled her arm through his, leading her to the room he'd come from. "I was getting worried. My other guests are already here. Did you have trouble finding the house?"

Karen shook her head, giving him a small smile. "I was afraid I missed the turn. I slowed down, probably more than I should have. I didn't mean to worry you, Mr. Troyington."

"Please, call me Bradford and it doesn't matter.

Night Angel

You're here now."

They turned as the front door opened. Karen's heart gave a small lurch as the man from the road walked in, dripping water on the gleaming black and white checkerboard marble floor. *I don't believe it. He's here!*

Bradford scowled as the new arrival smacked the butler's hand away. "Don't touch me," he growled.

The atmosphere in the hall changed, tension sparking along Karen's skin as she could almost feel Bradford's attitude turn as dark as the weather outside. She forced her voice to be light as she greeted the new arrival. "We meet again."

He glanced at her, giving her a curt nod, then opened a side pocket on the backpack and pulled out a small black plastic bag.

Bradford snatched it from him. "You know him?" he asked, not turning to look at her.

"I asked him for directions on the way here," she said, her gaze never leaving the face of the bedraggled stranger. "I'm Karen Spraiker."

"I know who you are," he said, his voice not betraying the anger she'd seen in his face a moment before.

Karen stared at him. He wasn't much taller than her own five foot, nine inch frame. His dripping clothes made him look thin, until she noticed the broad chest, the wide shoulders, the size of his arms. No bulges, just tightly corded muscles. What her father called workman's arms.

She smiled, trying to lift the mood surrounding them. "If I'd known you were coming here, I would've offered you a ride."

He dropped the backpack on the floor with a loud splat and yanked the zipper open. "I wouldn't have accepted. It's against Mr. Troyington's rules for any employee to mingle with the guests."

"Will you at least tell me your name?" Karen asked, needing to know.

He shifted his stare to Bradford, as if daring the rich man to stop him. "Randall Dupré."

"Where are you from?" The more he spoke to her, the more she felt a connection grow between them. Trying to get him to open up was another thing. And Bradford standing there looking daggers at him wasn't helping.

Randall pulled a few more items from the backpack, handing them to Bradford. "A small town in northern Louisiana you've probably never heard of."

Karen pushed harder, wanting to make him talk to her. "What are you doing in upstate New York? Isn't it a bit far from your home?"

Bradford jumped in. "He's here under special contract to me. Would you meet me in the library? I need to speak to my employee for a moment."

"Sure. It was nice meeting you," she said to Randall, before heading to the double doors. She hesitated at the doorway, then turned to get one more look at him. His wet clothes clung to his body like a second skin, allowing her to see all the lines and contours his clothing hid. She couldn't help staring at him, letting her mind wander in a direction that was sure to distract her from the "mystery" she was here to solve. As she gazed at him, she decided calmness and focus could take a hike where he was concerned.

She backed up a couple of steps to find a seat and

wait for her host when the sound of a slap snapped her back to the present. She flinched as Bradford struck Randall's face again. Karen's fingers curled into fists as she moved forward, her hero's instincts pushing her to intervene. As Bradford raised his hand again, Randall's arm shot out, grabbing Bradford's wrist. She drew in a breath, watching the muscles in his arm tighten as he forced his employer's arm down.

Randall grabbed the front of Bradford's shirt and jerked him close. His other hand balled as he drew his arm back. Bradford's mouth curled up in a mocking smile while he said something in a low voice. Randall let go and stepped back, shaking as his fingers curled into tight fists. The muscles in his neck tightened and veins popped out on his arm as Bradford spoke to him.

"I said, let's hear it," Bradford said, his voice raised loud enough for Karen to hear.

"I'm sorry, Mr. Troyington, for any problems I may have caused," Randall snapped, not sounding the least bit apologetic. "Please forgive me."

"Better. Now get to the basement. The sun's almost set, and I don't want you scaring the guests."

Karen held on to the door frame as Randall came closer to her, raising his gaze to hers. She'd stood watching, listening, perhaps a little longer than she should have. Water dripped from his hair into his eyes, but he didn't blink, didn't move. Karen's breathing faltered as they just stared at each other. He raised his hand, almost touching her face before snatching it back and stalking to the basement. The anger in his steps reverberated through her as he stormed away.

Karen backed into the library, settling herself on a small loveseat. What had Randall done to receive such harsh treatment? He wasn't happy about it, so why stand there and take it? Was Bradford this strict with all his staff? And why did Randall affect her like that? She shook her head. She'd just arrived and already had way too many questions. This was not the way to start a relaxing weekend.

She barely heard the background babble of the other guests as they mingled, wandering around the medium sized room. Glasses clinked and they laughed quietly. She closed her eyes. "Get a grip," she thought again.

An older woman with short, white hair and sparkling blue eyes walked over from near the doors and sat next to her. "Hello. I'm Edna. I don't remember seeing you here before. Is this your first murder mystery weekend?"

"Yes, it is," she said, turning to the woman. "Karen Spraiker. I won an invitation to come here from a contest. It came at the right time too. I was ready for a little R & R. How about you? Have you been here before?"

"Oh, yes. I come every year. I was a friend of Bradford's parents." Edna chuckled. "I was watching Bradford when he saw you. I think he likes you. He can't hide anything from these old eyes."

Karen smiled. "He just met me." Of course, it would be nice to have a handsome, rich guy fall in love with her. After all, it happened for her best friend, Misty, but she wasn't ready to jump back in the dating game just yet. And then there was Randall.

Edna nudged her lightly. "Sometimes that's all it takes. One look and before you know it, you're having a wedding."

Karen laughed. "Isn't that jumping the gun a little? I'm not looking for anyone right now. I'm just here to have fun."

"And fun you'll have," Bradford said, coming into the library. "I have a good mystery in store for you all. But that's for tomorrow. Right now, I've been informed dinner is ready."

Karen hung back, watching the group move to the dining room. There were only about ten or so and were mostly older folks. All of them had a look about them that made Karen wonder if they ran in Bradford's social circles. Movement outside caught her eye. She crossed to the floor length window, looking to her left, then right. She was sure something was out there. What had she seen?

"Ms. Spraiker, are you coming?" Bradford held his arm out to her.

"Yes. I thought I saw something. It was like a large bird." She looped her arm through his as they headed to the dining room. "And, please, call me Karen."

"You probably did. You're in the country, after all."

"That's reassuring. At least we know I'm not crazy." She smiled at her host, but her mind wouldn't quit. She'd never heard of any birds as big as what she thought she'd seen.

"Has Mr. Dupré worked for you long?" she asked, the question slipping out before she could stop herself.

Bradford frowned. "I regret bringing him here. He's more trouble than he's worth. If I didn't need him for a certain project, I'd send him packing."

She watched him frown as he talked about Randall, black emotions contorting his handsome features. Her combat instincts screamed at her, and she forced herself not to pull away. "Isn't there anyone else you can get? I mean, if he's such a problem, why keep him?"

"He has unique skills I require." He patted her hand. "Let's not talk about him any more. What do you think of my home so far?"

"It's very grand, with a style all its own." That style being gaudy, ostentatious, and totally overblown, she thought, looking at the ample supply of gold filigree, velvet drapes, and wall hangings making the large hall feel small and cramped. "I wanted to ask you if your butler is feeling okay. He's really pale."

To Karen's surprise, he laughed. "Jeffries is fine. He used to be in the theater. His father worked for my family. When his father died, Jeffries felt obligated to take over for him. Now, every year when I continue my parents' murder mystery tradition, he puts on his makeup to give the place atmosphere. I think he enjoys this as much as I do."

"Oh. He has a great touch. He really looks like he's on his last legs."

Bradford shrugged. "The skeletal look is a little cliché, but it works to get people in the mood for murder."

Voices drifted from the dining room, and she heard chairs scraping against the floor and the guests' voices as they talked. The heavy cloth in the hall was doing its best to absorb any sound that drifted its way.

"I can't wait for everything to start. I'm not sure what to expect, but it's bound to be exciting." She couldn't contain the excitement in her voice, nor did she want to. She could feel the tension leaving her shoulders the longer she was there. All she wanted was a good time and no worries.

Bradford smiled at her as they entered the brightly lit dining room, the guests seated all the way around with two empty places at the head of the table. He placed her on his left and moved to the end. Clearing his throat, he said, "I'd like to propose a toast. To our newest detective, Karen Spraiker. I wish her the best of luck when the mystery begins."

The guests raised their glasses, shouting, "Hear, hear."

Karen smiled, nodding her thanks at their show of support. Her thoughts strayed back to Randall. *Where is he now? Did he ever get dry?* Maybe he took a hot shower to warm up. She could almost see him peeling the wet jeans down his legs and pulling the soaked T-shirt off. Her cheeks flamed as she realized where her thoughts were leading her. She gulped down more wine to hide her embarrassment and forced herself to pay attention to the dinner conversation. This was going to be an interesting weekend, one way or the other.

Chapter Two

The morning sun streamed through the windows, brightening the hall and lighting the dining room with a golden glow. Karen inhaled the tantalizing aroma of eggs, bacon, toast, and coffee as she and the other guests walked around the buffet-style breakfast, choosing what they wanted, the silver pans sparkling as steam swirled upwards.

Excitement colored the conversation buzzing around her as she glanced at the guests. Bradford talked with Edna, seated to his right, as everyone helped themselves to coffee, tea, or orange juice and talked about what was to come.

"I can't wait for things to get hopping," an older gentleman said on her left, reaching for the coffee pot.

Jeffries came in, leaning down to whisper to his employer. Bradford stood and cleared his throat. "My butler has just informed me of a terrible crime. Our dear Mr. Lawrence has been viciously murdered and is currently lying on the floor of my study." Bradford smiled as the voices increased in volume. "Your adventure, ladies and gentlemen, has begun."

Silverware clattered on plates and chairs scraped against the floor as the group hurried to the study. There, Mr. Lawrence lay on the floor with a knife protruding from his chest, blood pooling around the blade. Karen bent for a closer look and saw the "victim" still breathing.

"Who would do such a thing?" she asked, getting into the spirit of the mystery.

"That's what you all will attempt to find out," Bradford said. "I will give you one tidbit to start with. All the clues will be found around the house, and anyone could be the killer, so be on your guard. Lunch will be served at two."

As the rest of the group dispersed, Bradford pulled Karen aside, kissing her cheek. "Good luck." He turned on his heel and left the room, leaving his guests to their own devices to solve the crime.

Karen smiled at his gesture. It was nice but didn't really do anything for her like Randall's icy gaze did. Just thinking about Randall made her heart pound. "Get a grip," she muttered. She bent down to retrieve a slip of paper from the "dead" man's jacket pocket.

"Shall we team up?"

Karen turned. Edna stood there, her mischievous smile lighting up her eyes.

"I suppose so. Are we allowed to work in teams?"

Edna nodded, offering her hand to Karen. "Of course. And with our combined talents, we'll surely win the prize at the end of the weekend."

"You're not just saying that to try and eliminate me later, are you?" Karen asked, raising an eyebrow.

Edna laughed, her voice bouncing around Karen like bubbles. "Don't be silly. We need each other. And I'll get even with Mrs. Donovan. She's won two years in a row. We'll show her what for."

Karen shook Edna's hand. "It's a deal." She pulled out the slip of paper. "Look what I found."

Edna rubbed her chin. "It looks like someone

wanted a meeting with him last night. And look over there." She pointed toward the french doors. "There's muddy foot prints on the rug."

Karen stepped carefully over the footprints to open the doors. "Let's check outside for clues."

The two women stepped out on the half circle stone porch. Karen inhaled deeply, savoring the crisp autumn air. Fall was her favorite season. The air had a freshness no other time of the year could claim. She shielded her eyes from the sun and looked at the woods encircling the property. The leaves were starting to turn color with an explosion of reds and golds, standing out brightly from the azure blue sky.

Edna pointed at footprints in front of one of the windows. "Someone was here."

"They go off that way." Karen headed to the corner of the house, Edna hard on her heels. "Listen." They heard the sound of chopping and slowed as they reached the end of the house. Peeking around the corner, Karen saw Randall splitting logs.

His arms tightened and rippled with every swing. It only took him one blow to split a large chunk of wood cleanly in two. He'd taken off his shirt, and it lay in the grass behind him, his tanned skin glowing in the morning light.

The warm October sun beat down on him, and his body glistened with the sweat of his labor, despite the chill breeze. His hair, blue-black in the bright sun, clung to his forehead, his faded blue jeans slung low on his hips. *Why isn't he wearing work gloves?* she wondered. His long fingers held the ax handle in a firm, comfortable grip.

A small shed stood behind him, housing wood for

the winter. A tall man wearing a heavy tool belt, his long, dark brown hair pulled into a ponytail, came out, wiping his hands on his jeans. He was at least six foot five with huge arms and wide shoulders. His A-line T-shirt was smudged with dirt and grease, and he looked at Randall like he was looking at a cockroach.

"Come on, Dupré," he shouted, his voice tinged with impatience. "You're not even halfway done with those logs, and there's a lot more to go."

Karen flinched as the ax came down hard enough to split the log and imbed itself in the block.

"It'd go faster if you'd help," he growled.

The man just smiled, stepping back inside the shed.

"Edna, would you excuse me a moment?" Not waiting for her partner's reply, Karen hurried over to Randall.

He straightened up at her approach. "Can I help you?"

There was that sexy, southern drawl again. Karen stared at the defined planes of his shoulders and chest, her gaze drifting to his waist. Realizing what she was doing, she forced her gaze back to his face. Someone had hit him hard enough to leave a large bruise on his cheek.

She cleared her throat. "I just wanted to apologize for getting you in trouble last night."

"It's all right. Troyington wasn't too mad." He lifted another piece of wood onto the block, hefting the ax in his hands. "Last night was nothing. He's usually worse." The ax whistled through the air, landing with a loud thunk in the wood.

His movements were smooth and fluid and becoming a real distraction. "Why do you stay if he treats you so badly? Isn't there someone you can report him to?"

"Report him?" A corner of his mouth lifted. "To who? I'm here of my own free will, under a contract of my own making."

Karen stared at the bruise on his cheekbone, trying to push away the compulsion to try and soothe it. "I don't understand..." Her voice died away as he stared at her.

The ice in his eyes darkened as he watched her face. "You can't. Not yet. The time isn't right."

Silence fell between them. Karen lifted her hand, overwhelmed by the need to touch his face.

His eyes softened, his lips quirking. "Don't worry about me, Ms. Spraiker. Worry about staying on Troyington's good side."

Slowly, he lifted his hand and brushed a thumb over her cheek. Karen caught her breath, unable to say a word. It was as if he felt her need to touch him, to be touched by him. At his touch, she could feel something powerful resonate in him. It felt *familiar* in a way.

"Solve your mystery and go home. Staying here is dangerous." He picked up the split wood, taking it to the shed. She gasped when he turned his back revealing ugly, red welts crisscrossing his shoulders.

****

Randall had sensed her approach even before he looked up to see her trotting across the yard. He hated the pity he saw written on her face. His biggest mistake was touching her. He should've kept his hands to himself. He'd forced himself not to flinch when he'd heard her gasp at the welts on his back. At least the bleeding had stopped. After he changed tonight, there wouldn't even be scars left. Cray, the handyman for the estate, stood watching him from the doorway to the shed.

"Move," Randall snarled. He stacked the logs along the back wall, then turned to get another load.

Cray folded his arms, leaning against the doorframe. "You're getting a little too familiar with that particular guest, Dupré. The boss isn't going to like it."

"You think I give a damn what Troyington likes? Think again." Randall pushed by him to bring in the first load he'd cut.

Cray watched Randall walk back and forth. "You need to show Mr. Troyington more respect."

"Respect?" Randall snorted. "Him? A man who kidnaps children for his own gain deserves no respect. Only whatever hell I can put him in."

Cray grabbed his arm, spinning him around. "Watch your mouth, southern boy."

"Or what?" Randall said, his eyes narrowing. "What do you think you can possibly do to me that you haven't done already?"

"How about this?" Cray slammed his fist into Randall's stomach, dropping him to one knee. "What's wrong, freak? Can't take a little hit?"

Randall raised his eyes to glare at Cray. "Oh, I can take it. Can you?" Randall surged to his feet, catching Cray with a right cross, knocking him backward into the tool rack. He rammed his shoulder into Cray's midsection, knocking the breath from the larger man. He slammed Cray's head against the peg board, making tools fall to the dirt floor with solid thuds. Cray wiped the blood from his mouth as Randall grabbed the front of his shirt, slamming him again into the tool rack as he drew his arm back.

"Wait," Cray cried out, throwing his hands up in front of him. "You haven't really thought about what you're doing, have you?"

Randall hesitated, then let him go, stepping back. *No*, he thought, *I haven't. People are depending on me, and I let Cray get under my skin.*

Cray smiled, drawing himself up to tower over Randall. "Mr. Troyington's going to find out about this. Then you won't be so smug, will you? If he didn't need you and whatever power you claim you possess, I'd break your neck and leave you here."

Randall's hands curled into fists, itching to wipe the smug smirk off Cray's face. "But he does. How would he feel if his guests found out what he's really doing here? Rich people don't like being associated with illegal experimentation. The only reason I haven't told them is because I want to make sure you keep your hands off the children."

Cray poked him hard in the chest. "That's right. You cooperate and everyone stays healthy. You haven't forgotten that, have you?"

Randall squeezed his eyes shut. He remembered the faces of the pack as they had asked for his help. He'd felt the fury radiate from Caledon even though his outward appearance had been calm. Their children were their future and both were in danger. He was supposed to keep them safe, not lose his temper because of men like Cray. No. He hadn't forgotten.

"Did you, Dupré?" Cray said, biting off the end of every word.

"No. I didn't." He glared at Cray, his lip pulling up in a snarl. If he could get away with it, Cray wouldn't be walking out of the shed.

"The brats live so long as you keep in line. Another outburst like this and he may make an example of one. Maybe even the pack leader's son. That wouldn't look too good for you, now would it?"

Randall took a step toward him. "Don't hurt them," he said through clenched teeth.

Cray shoved him hard, making him stumble back a few steps. "Then you'd better start behaving yourself."

Randall glared at him, inwardly pleased to see a little bit of fear fill Cray's eyes. "Know this. Troyington and the rest of you only live by my discretion. Once I find the children, don't count on another sunrise."

Cray shook himself then stood straighter, looking down at Randall and shoving him again. "Big talk for a little man."

Randall snorted as he looked the larger man over. "I'm not impressed."

Cray swung his fist, knocking Randall to the ground. "One of these days, I'm not going to wait for the okay. I'm just going to get rid of you."

Randall spit blood on the floor and wiped his mouth. "Funny, I was just thinking the same thing about you."

Cray kicked him as he went by. "Get back to work, and remember, I'm keeping an eye on you the whole time."

Randall pushed himself to his feet, rubbing his side. His knuckles were bleeding again. He turned his hand over to look at his palm. Damn. The blister between his thumb and forefinger was back. Add in the dirt, cuts, scrapes, splinters, and everything else he'd picked up and he was a real mess. He shook his head.

This was the hand he'd laid on Karen's cheek.

He hadn't stopped thinking about her since he'd first seen her. He swung the ax, seeing her face with those beautiful brown eyes, the high cheekbones, the full lips. Her skin was softer than he thought it would be. The dragon spirit coiled in her and surged to life with his touch. He had noticed the dragon pendant she wore and knew it connected her to the creatures of old. She had accepted their power but hadn't set it loose yet. It filled her and made her strong. He could still feel the power from her tingle in his fingertips.

He gazed in the direction she had gone. Should he make his move soon? He allowed himself a small smile. Hell, Marshall probably would've smacked him in the head by now and demanded to know what he was waiting for.

Randall had no doubt Cray would run straight to Troyington to relate the morning's events. He split another log, turning to spit more blood on the ground. *Have I endangered the children?* he thought. As the ax whistled down, he wished more than ever to find the werewolf children and go back to his own clan. Karen's face filled his mind. Would she go with him if he asked her? Or would she turn from him when she saw his other side?

****

Karen had wanted to reach out to him when she saw the welts on his back. But he walked away, leaving her not knowing what to do. She wondered about the power she could still feel from him and why it seemed it was an important part of her. Not wanting Edna to know what she was thinking, she asked brightly, "Shall we continue?"

"Do you know Randall Dupré?" Edna asked.

She glanced toward the shed. "I just met him yesterday. I thought I was lost, and he gave me directions. I wanted to thank him." *I feel like I've known him forever. How can this be?*

"You'd do well to stay away from him. Bradford doesn't like his help to talk to the guests." Edna pulled Karen in the direction they'd been heading.

Karen frowned as her companion hurried her away from where Randall was working. "Oh? Why?"

"The Troyingtons are an old family with old beliefs. Servants are below them." Edna looped her arm through Karen's. "That Dupré character is suspicious. You can see it in his eyes."

Karen thought about Randall's eyes. They were magical, the color of ice lit by an inner fire. Her breath quickened as his face planted itself clearly in her mind. Her spirit longed for him and cried out as she moved farther away from him. She realized Edna was speaking again.

Edna took a wary glance over her shoulder. "There's something spooky about him. He seems to have taken a liking to you, but don't let him get too close."

Karen focused on controlling what she wanted to say. She couldn't remember the last time she'd had to remind herself so many times to remain calm and focused. "He doesn't strike me as a maniac or anything, and he doesn't scare me."

"You're young, my dear." Edna patted her hand. "Just make sure you keep your distance. Now, if you need someone, I'm pretty sure Bradford wouldn't mind filling the job."

"Are you trying to play matchmaker?" Karen teased.

"Heavens, no." Edna winked at her. "But if you want me to, I will."

Karen shook her head, wishing Edna would let the subject drop. "I'm not in the market right now. I'm just here for an enjoyable weekend."

She thought of Bradford with his blond hair and chiseled good looks. She'd have nothing to worry about for the rest of her life if she hooked up with him, but Randall's image took over Bradford's in her mind. He was used to hard work and, from the condition his clothes were in, didn't have much money. When he'd laid his hand on her cheek, she'd felt its roughness even though his caress had been gentle.

Bradford was used to being in charge and not having his orders questioned. Randall had fire in his soul, yet did nothing to stand up for himself. *What's wrong with him?* she wondered. *Is he a coward? Why?* There had to be a reason. No man would willingly take such abuse.

Things at the estate weren't adding up. Karen knew there was a real mystery here and not just the one staged for their benefit.

Chapter Three

The guests gathered in the drawing room after dinner, their excitement palpable as they discussed the day's events. A fire crackled merrily, taking the chill out of the air, its glow adding warmth to the light from the table lamps. Shadows danced in the corners, and Karen avoided looking at them and the guests who cast them, preferring to stare out the window, trying to catch a glimpse of what she'd seen the night before.

"Well done, everyone," Bradford said, entering the room. "Some of you are on the right track. Keep up the good work."

He moved to stand behind Karen. "Are you enjoying yourself?"

"Yes, I am, very much. It's fun to be part of a mystery, not just watching or reading about one." She turned back to the darkness, wishing he'd go talk to the others.

He raised his eyebrows as he gazed at her, then turned to stare out the window with her. "Looking for something in particular out there?"

"Not really. I was hoping to catch another glimpse of whatever I saw last night."

He smiled. "Good luck. It may not even be in the area any more."

Karen wanted to see for herself. She laid her hand on the glass, wanting to know what lay in the darkness beyond. "Would it be all right if I took a walk outside? Just for a little bit?"

"Only if I can come with you."

"Of course." Karen smiled, swallowing her disappointment. She'd wanted some time alone. Hopefully the giant bird wouldn't be scared by two of them. She felt she would've had a better chance of seeing it if she were by herself.

Bradford opened the french doors and guided her outside into the darkness beyond, steering her off to the right. "The gardens are around this way. You won't be able to see much at night, but you can get an idea of how large they are."

"I'm sure they're beautiful." Finding the bird was foremost in her mind, not the gardens. Of course, it'd be nice finding Randall, too. "You'll have to give me a tour of them when the sun's up."

"I'd love to show you around tomorrow after the mystery is over, if you have time before you leave." He pulled her arm through his.

"We'll see." Karen's gaze wandered over the outside of the house. "You really do have a lovely home." At least the exterior wasn't as gaudy as the interior.

"Thank you." He stared at his home, not saying anything for a few moments. "My parents worked hard to make this place what it is. When my mother became ill, my father had the balcony built all the way around the house for her. She couldn't manage the stairs, but she still loved to go outside."

She laid her hand on his arm. "Your father must've loved her very much."

Bradford nodded. "After her death, he gave me this

house and moved back to England. My mother stipulated in her will that I continue to hold our annual murder mystery weekend. She didn't want to see the tradition die. Our family has held these for many years."

Karen looked at him. "You don't seem like you don't want to do it."

He stared at the house. "I just don't have the heart for it any more. My mother always ran it."

"Then why continue? Surely your father knows how you feel about it."

"He does, but there's nothing we can do. If I stop, the house and grounds revert to my brother and neither of us wants that to happen." He shook his head. "This year is a bad time. I have some companies in the middle of groundbreaking research and to have guests here takes my attention away from important business matters."

Is that how Randall figured into all of this? Maybe that was why Bradford treated him so badly. It was more than likely too much of everything all at the same time. When she felt overwhelmed, she meditated to clear her mind to get her emotions back under control. To break her calm, especially in front of others, she felt, would show a weak spirit.

Karen studied Bradford in the moonlight. He had everything, good looks, money, style, grace, people to do his bidding. He'd shown interest in her as soon as he'd seen her. So why didn't he make her heart race like Randall did? What was wrong with her? Did she just need to give him and herself a little more time?

Karen's gaze skimmed the trees and the area around them. She could feel something watching her and Bradford but couldn't see it in the darkness. *Could it be the huge bird?* she thought. She narrowed her eyes and tried harder to see in the inky black of the woods.

"What are you thinking about?" Bradford asked.

She inhaled the perfect October air as she hesitated, not wanting him to know her true thoughts. "I love the woods in the fall," she finally said.

"I can tell," he said, pulling her closer and wrapping an arm around her shoulders. "You haven't stopped staring at the trees since you arrived."

"It's because..." She stopped short. "You'll think I'm being childish."

"Try me. I won't laugh." He laid his left hand over his heart and raised his right. "I promise."

She glanced toward the trees. "When I was little, I used to think fairies were responsible for the leaves changing colors. I'd go into the woods by our house to look for them. My brother used to tease me about it." She shrugged. "I guess part of me still wants fairies to be real."

"It's not childish. It's sweet." He stared at her in the moonlight. "Are you sure you're not one of them?"

Karen playfully slapped his chest. "Stop it. You said you wouldn't laugh."

"I'm sorry." He turned her toward him. "I simply meant you're as beautiful as a fairy."

"Thank you." Her eyes wandered to the ground, the trees, the gardens, anywhere but to the man in front of her.

As he leaned closer to kiss her, his handyman hurried across the ground. "Mr. Troyington, we have a problem."

Bradford stepped back and turned to him. "What's

wrong, Cray?"

Cray hesitated and glanced at Karen. "We couldn't hold him, and he got out before we could lock him up."

"Find him," Bradford said. "Let him know he's pushing his luck."

Cray nodded. "You know you should've put him in the other facility."

Karen looked at both men. "What's going on? Who's pushing his luck?"

Bradford held his hand up as a quiet flapping sounded, growing steadily louder. A huge shadow covered the moon, hung in the air for a split second, then dove at them, the wind screaming over its wings. Bradford threw Karen to the ground, and Cray dropped down as whatever it was peeled off toward the tree line.

He raised his head, looking for the creature. "I think we found your large bird."

Karen sat up, brushing leaves and grass from her jacket. "I think you're right," she said with a shaky laugh.

Bradford eyed the sky, scowling. "We'd better get back to the house." He turned to Cray. "Let Harmon know about this and take care of the situation."

Cray nodded and ran off as they jogged back to the squares of light spilling from the mansion's windows. Karen stopped on the porch, turning back to the darkness. What was all that about? She had a feeling that Cray and Bradford were talking about Randall. What facility did they mean? And why did Bradford have such a look of concern on his face after Cray told him? Once again, too many questions. He gave her a gentle, yet insistent, push into the drawing room, locking the doors behind them.

"What do you think it is?" she asked.

The guests turned to them.

"Did something happen?" Edna asked.

"We intruded on a large bird's nesting place," Bradford said. "It let us know in no uncertain terms we weren't welcome there."

Karen stared at him. "That thing was huge. Are you sure it's a bird?" Bradford's explanation was a little too quick, like he knew what it was that dove at them.

"Most birds, especially the ones in this area, are much bigger than people realize." He took her hands in his. "I sent Cray to my stable master to have him go look for it. In the morning, he can relocate it to another area on the estate."

She glanced at the window, her knees still shaking. "That might be best. If you don't mind, I think I'm going to turn in," she said, heading for the door.

Bradford reached out, capturing her hand. "It's still early. Are you sure you don't want to stay a little longer?"

"I'm sure. I'm tired and I need to make a phone call." She gave him a quick smile as she pulled her hand from his. "Too much excitement for one evening."

He walked her to the door. "Good night. I'll see you in the morning."

She nodded to the guests as they wished her sweet dreams. Her feet carried her swiftly up the staircase and down to her room. She sighed when she finally locked herself away from everyone, especially her host. She'd been relieved when they were interrupted before he kissed her.

She sat on the bed and closed her eyes. She took three deep breaths and relaxed every muscle, focusing on the still pond in her mind she used to center herself. She opened her eyes and looked around the room. The art on the walls of nature scenes eased her jumbled feelings.

The glass on the french doors to the balcony were frosted and had animals etched into them. Sheer, ivory curtains covered the windows and balcony doors; heavier tan drapes pulled to the sides. A natural wood chair rail divided the wall in half, light green at the top and dark green at the bottom.

She smiled and nodded. Now, she felt more like herself. Pulling out her cell phone, she hit the speed dial for home and kicked off her shoes.

"Angel Haven, Ariel speaking. May I help you?"

"Hey, it's Karen. Is Kristin there?"

"Dr. Mentor has been called out of town on business. Is there anyone else you wish to speak to?"

"Who's home?" Karen walked to the balcony doors. Pushing the curtains aside, she tried again to find whatever it was flying around the estate.

"Mrs. McClennan is here visiting. Would you like to speak to her?"

Karen had actually wanted Kristin's steady advice, but Misty could give her some insight about what was going on. "Sure. Put her on."

"One moment, please."

Karen chewed her bottom lip while she waited. With all Misty had been through lately, she was sure to have some advice on how to handle Bradford.

"Karen, it's been forever."

"It's only been a couple of months since you left, and you're still at the mansion more often than not." Karen walked back to the bed and stretched out, crossing her ankles. "And didn't we just fight part of Medusa's team earlier this week?"

"You have no flair for the dramatic. How have you been?"

Karen thought about that for a moment. After Misty's marriage, she had battled jealousy, hurt, and loneliness. Finding her center after that had been harder than she thought. "Okay, I guess. We all miss you around Angel Haven. How's married life?"

"Great. The only downside is that he's gone on assignments so much. Every time Commander Frailer needs an ULTRA rep, he sends Jack."

Karen could hear the exasperation in her friend's voice. "Your fault for marrying someone so popular."

"Tell me about it. I swear, if one more female rookie agent bats her eyes at him, it's going to be POW, right to the moon."

Karen couldn't stop the laugh that pushed its way out. *Maybe I don't have a reason to be jealous after all.* Poor Misty. She certainly had her hands full. Her husband Jack was way too hot with his long red hair, perfect physique, and slight British accent. ULTRA's top field commander was certainly in the best shape of anyone she'd ever seen. And marriage hadn't changed Misty one bit. "You were the one who proclaimed him drop-dead gorgeous," Karen said. "This is the price you have to pay."

"Ooh, thanks for the sympathy."

"Hang on a second, while I wring the sarcasm out of my phone."

"So, did you call just to bust my chops, or are you homesick? Kristin said you were on a weekend getaway."

Karen pushed the speaker button on her phone and sat up to braid her hair. "Neither. I just need to talk to someone."

"Shoot. I'll try to help."

She twisted a rubber band around the end, then threw her suitcase on the bed and flipped it open. "The guy who owns the mansion I'm staying in is interested in me. His name is Bradford Troyington."

"Nice. Tell me more."

Karen pulled out her nightshirt and a pair of sweat pants. "He's got a huge house, people that work for him, and he's worth about a zillion dollars. His family goes back generations."

"So far, so good," Misty said. "Please continue."

Karen yanked her nightshirt over her head. "After what happened with the horrible relationship I've just gotten out of, I don't want anyone right now. And Bradford's kind of harsh to his people." She paused. "Well, one of his people."

"I see," Misty said. "Well, you're coming home tomorrow, right? You could always take advantage of the situation. After all, you'll probably never see him again."

Karen plopped on the bed. "You know I can't do that. I don't want to hurt his feelings. And there's this other guy here."

"Uh oh. I'm sensing a problem."

She yanked her socks off and shoved them under the night table next to the bed. "Misty, you should see him. He's not big, like Jack, but he's no slouch either. And he's got the most beautiful eyes. He would definitely make your list of guys not going to heaven because what they do to a pair of pants is a sin."

Misty laughed. "Well, Jack is number one on the list now. I'd like to see this other guy to make sure he's list worthy."

Karen grabbed her fuzzy, boot-shaped slippers and pulled them on. "His name's Randall. When he looks at me, I swear, my knees actually go weak."

"You don't get weak knees. You're the steadiest person I know." Karen could picture Misty shrugging as she spoke. "If you're using terms like 'weak knees,' Randall could be the one for you."

"Randall is one of Bradford's servants. He's not allowed to speak to me, and people keep warning me away from him." Karen sighed. "So much for my relaxing weekend. It's weird, because I feel there's something big going on here. I just can't figure it out."

"You have pretty good instincts about people," Misty said. "What does your gut tell you?"

"That he's not a bad guy." Karen sat up, turning her gaze to the darkness looming outside. "But here's the wrinkle. Randall says Bradford is dangerous." She padded to the balcony doors. "And there's this huge bird that keeps flying around the mansion."

"You just lost me with the bird. How is that relevant to two guys?"

"Because I think it's back. I just heard something outside my window. I'll call you later." Karen snapped the phone shut and opened the door a crack, looking along the platform encircling the house. Nothing.

She stepped out, heading straight for the rail and leaned over. Again, nothing. She leaned against the support beam. "I know I heard something out here," she murmured.

"Are you looking for me?" a gravelly voice said,

sounding right next to her.

Karen shrieked as she jumped, feeling her heart trying to pound its way through her chest. She stared into the large tree growing next to the house. Its thick branches hung over the low roof. The voice came from there.

She backed toward the door to her room. "Not unless you're a huge bird."

"Be calm," the voice said. "I mean you no harm. And no, I'm not a bird."

"Show yourself," she demanded. Her back hit the wall, stopping her cold.

"To my regret, I can't. I don't think you'd understand."

"Understand what?" She took a deep breath and, trembling, inched her way back to the rail. Calm, she thought. Focus. You're not defenseless.

"Who I am. What I am." The tree branch bobbed as she heard him move to another spot.

She peered through the leaves. Something large and shadowy sat back by the trunk and she couldn't tell exactly it was. "That doesn't make any sense."

"I know." A rumbling laugh floated from the tree top. "I'm a guardian, a night angel if you will. I protect those who can't protect themselves."

"What are you doing here?" Karen craned her neck to see toward the top. She hadn't even heard him move.

"My charges were stolen from me. They are naught but children. I intend to find them and take them home."

Karen cringed from the determination in his voice. She pitied whoever it was that crossed him. "I'm sorry."

"So will the person be who took them." More rustling as the speaker moved again. Karen moved with him, still trying to see.

"Is there anything I can do to help?"

Silence. "I don't think so," he finally said.

Even with the amount of leaves that had fallen, enough remained to hide whoever was there. And why was she out here talking to someone she couldn't see anyway? Had she lost her mind? "You know, this is a little much." *I know I'm a superhero, but this is crazy.*

"I know this is hard for you. I understand if you don't believe me. But don't trust Troyington. He's not what he seems."

Karen crossed her arms. "Someone else told me that today. It would be easier to trust you if I could see you."

"Listen to Randall. He knows what he's talking about." The voice came from a different spot again.

She frowned. "You know Randall Dupré?" How did he know who she meant?

The voice chuckled. "Oh yes. Randall and I have been acquainted for years. He offered his assistance to me. He's gathering information."

Her blood pounded in her veins as anger ripped through her. Bright light flared behind her eyes, and she felt something inside her straining to be set free. "Do you know what he's going through for you?" Her hands clenched into fists. "He's been beaten. He's been abused. Why don't you go help *him*?"

"Calm yourself. I know everything Randall has suffered since he came here three months ago." The voice now sounded sad. "There is nothing I can do for him in the daylight."

Karen sagged against the railing and pressed her hand to her forehead. "I'm sorry. I don't lose my temper like that. Not ever. I keep myself under control all the time. I just can't stand what I've seen of his treatment."

"But you spend your time with Troyington."

Karen stared at the tree. Why did it sound like he was disappointed in her? "He likes me. I think he wants me to like him."

"And yet..." Amusement colored the words of the invisible speaker.

"There's something about Randall that calls out to me. I just met the man yesterday." Karen crossed her arms, rubbing them, not sure if it was the chill in the air or her nerves making goose bumps run along her arms. "Bradford is everything a girl is supposed to want. Randall is the one I think about. Is that weird?"

"No. The fairies would say you found your soul mate."

"I thought soul mates were only in romance novels or movies." Karen wanted to believe he was making fun of her, but the truth of his words penetrated her soul. She trembled harder. *You* know *you and Randall are soul mates,* a little voice whispered to her heart.

"Soul mates are very real. They've been around since the beginning of man. Souls are precious things. When two who are destined to be together meet, a powerful bond is formed. The fairy folk have known that for centuries." The amusement in his voice was back. "Humans can be a little slow on the uptake."

Karen threw her hands up. "Hold it a second. Did you just say fairies are real?"

"Of course. You've known it for years. They've

been keeping an eye on you. They're glad you still believe in them. Unfortunately, you told Troyington."

Karen shook so hard, she felt like a mini earthquake. "Have I endangered them?"

"No. They can take care of themselves. They always have."

She leaned on the rail, needing to hold herself up. "How do you know all this?"

"Because," the voice whispered. "I'm one of them."

Karen's stomach dropped when large wings beat the air. The speaker took to the sky, and was gone.

Chapter Four

Randall jerked awake as ice cold water splashed over his face and naked chest. He struggled as rough hands yanked him off his bed and threw him to the concrete floor. He wiped the water from his eyes and shoved his hair back. Troyington loomed over him along with Cray and a man wearing a green turtleneck, dark brown pants, and a flat cap over his dark, wavy hair. Randall frowned. If Troyington brought Harmon, the stable master, and Cray, things were about to get ugly.

Troyington dropped the plastic bucket on the hard floor with a dull thud. "Get up, Dupré," he snapped as Cray and Harmon jerked him to his feet.

Randall spit water on the floor and stood, glaring at Troyington. "What do you want this time?"

Troyington nodded to Cray and the man slammed his fist into Randall's stomach. "You do not now or *ever* lay a hand on my employees. Is that understood?"

Randall dropped to the floor, holding his midsection as he gasped for breath. "Why? Can't they fight their own battles?"

Troyington gestured to Harmon. The stable master hauled Randall to his feet, holding his arms behind him as Cray landed several solid blows to his face. Randall felt his nose break and wondered if he was going to lose teeth this time. Teeth seemed to take forever to regenerate. He pulled against the stable master and got another punch from Cray for his efforts.

Troyington raised his hand. "Bring him."

Cray and Harmon dragged Randall down a familiar hallway. He winced as his feet scraped against the concrete floor, which meant his toes were going to be raw by the time they got to their destination. *At least I've got my pants this time*, he thought.

Blood dripped from his face, leaving a splotchy trail down the otherwise pristine hallway. He gave a small shake of his head. He should've known this was going to happen. Back to the room.

Cray and Harmon threw him into the small concrete room he'd occupied when Troyington had first found out what he was. His shoulder slammed painfully into the far wall, the rough concrete leaving raw scratches on his skin. The two men grabbed him again, turning him around for their employer's inspection. Randall flinched when Troyington's fingers probed his back.

"Amazing," Troyington said. "Yesterday morning, I had you bleeding. Today, you're perfectly healed. It's like you were never touched." He turned to his men. "Get Dr. Strathmore. Tell her to get me a blood sample while he's human, one during the transformation, and one when the change is complete."

"Just what are you looking for?" Randall said, his broken nose making him sound like he was clogged with a cold.

Troyington smiled but his eyes were hard. "I want the power you and those werewolf brats have. As a shape-shifter, I'll have heightened senses. After determining how much of your blood I need, I'll have regeneration. All of which I'll be able to use against my business rivals."

"It's enhanced senses," Randall said, condescension dripping from his words. "Not telepathy."

Troyington shook his head. "You just don't understand. Being able to hear rapid heartbeats, see small facial changes, smell fear, that's what will give me the edge."

Randall's eyes widened as the full impact of Troyington's words hit him. With the power of a shape-shifter, the enhanced senses would actually make his business sense sharper. It would complement him better than psionics. He'd acquire more and more power, until there was no one left to challenge him. *Great*, Randall thought. *Another nut job with a take-over-the-world scheme.*

Having seen Troyington's reaction to Karen every time she was near him, Randall threw another barb at the rich man. "What do you think Ms. Spraiker will say about this? Do you think she'll just stand by and watch you grab all that power?"

Randall knew his statement hit home and smiled as Troyington's face turned bright red, his face pulling down into a dark scowl. He'd take a small victory over no victory any day.

Troyington crossed over to him, slapping him hard across the face, sending new waves of pain through Randall's nose. "What do you think she'll say when she finds out you're not even human? Why not show her the monster you are in the dark?"

Randall scowled as fresh blood dripped from his face. When would he learn to keep his mouth shut?

Apparently not now. "And yet, you want to be one of us."

"Yes, I do." Troyington kicked Randall's right knee out from under him, making him cry out as white hot pain lanced through his leg. He raised watering eyes to his captor. Troyington stood over Randall, his voice low and menacing. "And if I have to go through all of you guardians and every werewolf brat in North America to get that ability, rest assured, I will."

Cray and Harmon stood over Randall as Troyington headed toward the hall. He looked at the two men. "I have to be upstairs for breakfast. Take him to the barn and make sure this time, he doesn't get away from you. Give me ten minutes before you leave."

After Troyington stalked from the room, the two men checked their watches several times before nodding and grabbing him again. They quickly hauled him outside and down the hill that obscured the barn from the view from the house. They shoved him in the small storage room at the end of the stalls where horses whinnied, letting the men know they didn't appreciate the interruption.

They left him there, slamming the door shut. Randall limped across the room, staring at the door that stood between him and freedom. It had been lined with a thin layer of a dull metal, and the wood on all the walls had been treated the same way. He touched his finger to the surface, jerking his hand back as if he'd been burned. The skin bubbled on his fingertip. Cold iron. Werewolves had silver, vampires had holy relics, his people had cold iron. None in the fairy realm could withstand being near the metal.

He thought about what the High Mother had told

him before he left. Troyington's men had paranormal abilities, just as he figured. Cray had superhuman strength. Randall was lucky the man was more of a coward that enjoyed bullying than an actual fighter. Harmon could speak to any animal on earth, which was where Troyington's men got a lot of their information. The very creatures that lived with the fairies had unknowingly betrayed them. And Troyington could recognize magic and sense when it was being used. He couldn't wield magic, but he knew when someone else did.

Randall looked around at his small cell. He couldn't get away from the metal on the walls and the door and just the scent of it was making his stomach turn. He needed to get out of there and warn the kids. He wanted to see Karen. Right now, though, Troyington held all the cards. *"Damn him!"*

He walked to the middle of the room and sat cross legged on the floor. He swallowed hard to stop the nausea rising in the back of his throat. The metal was dulling his senses and as blood from his nose dripped in his lap, he knew it was also slowing his healing ability.

****

"Good morning, everyone." Bradford smiled as he entered the dining room. "Eat hearty. Today, we must have a solution to the mystery."

Karen carried her plate to the table, sitting next to Edna. "Do you think we'll have it figured out before the others?"

"Of course. We've almost got it now." Edna winked at her. "A few more clues to solidify what we know, and it's in the bag."

Karen smiled at Edna as she patted the older

woman's hand. "I've enjoyed our partnership. It's been fun getting to know you."

"Same here, dear. Are you finished?" At Karen's nod, Edna stood. "Let's get down to business."

Karen followed Edna into the hall. "Should we check the basement today?" she asked. "I know the others have already been down there, but they may have missed something."

"Sounds like a good place to start." Edna led the way to the cellar door.

The two women flipped on the light switch and descended the stairs. Karen looked around in amazement. "This doesn't look like any basement I've ever seen." The hallway and doors were all stark white. Nothing was out of place. The lights were startlingly bright. Everything looked almost sterile in its cleanliness. "It's more like a hospital."

"Bradford likes every area in his home to be tidy. Nothing out of place," Edna said at her elbow. "You start on that side. Holler if you see anything."

"I will." Karen opened the first door, finding only a storage closet filled with cleaning supplies. Poking through the items, she discovered one of the "victim's" cigarettes and a fancy silver button. She pocketed both, heading to the next door a little further down. That room was just a storage closet for holiday decorations. Finding nothing useful in there, she continued on. The third door made her stop.

It was locked tight. Karen pushed on it a little harder, but it wouldn't budge. She wondered why that one was locked up. She looked down and saw what looked like tiny drops of blood on the floor. They went down the hall to her left.

She glanced around for Edna but didn't see the older woman. Curiosity getting the better of her, she followed the trail down a long corridor running the length of the mansion. The droplets stopped at a large metal door. She reached out a hand, hesitating only briefly before yanking on the handle. It opened easily, throwing her off balance.

She stepped inside and looked around. The room was completely barren and didn't have the look of the rest of the basement. Whitewashed cinder block walls held a chill she hadn't felt anywhere else. The droplets were in here and just stopped. *Who was here?* she wondered. What happened to them? What was going on in this house?

She took another deep breath, but this time, it didn't help. She turned to leave, and her eyes widened when she saw the walls. Gouges marred the walls to either side of the door and the dark brown stain covering them could've been dried blood.

She went back to the hallway and Edna was there. "Did you find anything?"

Karen shook her head. "No. That room was empty. It looked like there was blood on the floor. Was someone hurt?"

Edna smiled. "It could've been Cray. This room used to be a workshop for Bradford's father. Cray sometimes uses it when he needs more space."

"But it's so cold in there."

Edna nodded. "I know. Cray only uses it in the summer when the outside temperatures get too high. He may have been in here the other day and cut himself. That's probably what you saw."

Karen watched Edna shut the door and make sure it

was closed tight. "There are gouges on the walls by the door that look like claw marks and a stain that looks a lot like blood."

Edna shrugged. "It's entirely possible. I'm not sure what Cray does down there, and I think it's best not to ask him. I wouldn't understand anything he says anyway. He's all about carpentry and mechanics and things an old lady like me doesn't know anything about. Let's get back upstairs. I need to ask Bradford a few things, and you look like you need something to drink."

Karen got herself a cup of hot tea and sat in a tapestry chair in the hallway. She watched the other guests walk about, make notes in little notebooks, and confer. She sipped her tea. She was feeling better. She'd be a lot better if she could just grab Randall and run. She nodded to two gentlemen who stopped in front of her, silently willing them to move.

She thought about Randall and where he could possibly be. She wanted to try to see him again, and the mystery would be over this afternoon. The events of the previous day came back to her. She'd spoken with him, and he'd touched her cheek. Her eyes closed as she remembered the feel of his hand on her face. His skin was rough, and she'd seen the blisters. But his touch had been feather light, almost like he'd been afraid to touch her.

She worried about the welts on his back. He needed to be seen by a doctor. She felt her power flare again. She didn't understand what was happening with it, but every time she thought of Randall and his touch, her power reacted. *You know why you have strong feelings for him,* the little voice inside her whispered again. *Just believe it.*

"Are you feeling any better?" Karen jumped as Edna laid a hand on her shoulder. She hadn't even heard her approach. "I believe everyone is heading for the dining room."

The cup clinked against the china saucer as Karen's hands shook. "I'm sorry. I got lost in my own little world for a minute."

Edna grinned at her, giving her a little nudge. "Quite all right. I think we have the right solution. I can't wait until after lunch when we make our revelation."

Karen thought about all the explanations Edna had given her in the basement. They all seemed to be plausible, but something about them sat sour with her. There were too many secrets, too many lies floating around. Karen was beginning to wish the weekend was over. Edna appeared so nice, so normal. For a brief moment, she wished she'd never accepted the invitation to come.

****

The guests assembled in the drawing room after lunch. Bradford clapped his hands for their attention. "All right. It's time to make our guesses and unmask the murderer. Who would like to go first?"

Karen half listened as the guests made their suppositions. Her thoughts were on a certain southern man who was far from home and putting up with things he shouldn't have to because a friend needed his help. Could she be that strong? She'd been through some pretty tough times in the past and had taken a few on the chin for her friends, but nothing like this. She wanted more time to talk to Randall. She just didn't know how she was going to get it.

Karen glanced at Edna out of the corner of her eye. Could the older woman be lying? But why? What reason did she have? Karen wished she was staying longer to get the answers she wanted.

Edna nudged her, snapping her back to the current conversation. "We have the right answer, don't we, Karen?"

"What? Yes, we believe we have the correct solution." At Edna's nod, Karen stood up, revealing the bits of evidence they had. "We found this note in the dead man's jacket, claiming he was to have a meeting with whoever killed him. There were muddy footprints on the floor the morning after the murder. We followed the trail around the house to the basement door. This morning, we found the victim's brand of cigarettes and a button matching the butler's uniform." Karen paused, taking a deep breath before continuing. "Everything we found leads us to the conclusion that, and I can't believe I'm saying this, the butler did it."

Jeffries stood in the corner of the room. He cleared his throat. "Egad, sir. I've been found out."

Bradford clapped and approached the two of them. He hugged Karen, holding her for a few extra heartbeats while the guests applauded them. "Very good, Karen," he whispered. He stood back, keeping Karen's hand trapped in his. "Congratulations, ladies. You've got the correct solution and will get the prize."

"What is it this time?" Edna's eyes sparkled with anticipation.

"You will each get five thousand dollars in cash. Is that good enough for you, my dear Edna?" Bradford leaned down to kiss her cheek.

"That's lovely."

Karen's eyes opened wide. "That's awfully generous of you, but isn't it a bit much?"

"That's a drop in the bucket for our Bradford," Edna said.

Bradford gave her a wink. "Trust me, Karen. If I'd miss it, I wouldn't have offered it."

Karen waited for the shiver to run through her when Bradford said her name. Nothing. How could Randall affect her like that and not Bradford? Was her nighttime visitor right? Were she and Randall soul mates even though they'd barely spoken? Was there such a thing as love at first sight?

"I want to thank you all for coming again this weekend," Bradford was saying. "Next year should be even grander."

The group filed out, the guests disappearing into other rooms and upstairs to gather belongings.

Bradford held Karen's hand. "I'm glad you and Edna solved the mystery," he said.

Karen smiled at him. "I had a lot of fun doing it. Working with Edna was great." Karen knew she ought to be flattered by Bradford's attention to her, but one question nagged at her.

Where was Randall?

Chapter Five

The afternoon sun sank behind the trees, giving the woods a warm glow as the guests said their goodbyes to their host. Karen stood on the porch next to Bradford, waiting for her turn to bid him farewell. Her gaze wandered across the grounds, trying to find Randall, but he was nowhere to be seen. Bradford kept a tight grip on her hand as she turned to him.

"Thanks again for a wonderful weekend," she said. "I hope you'll have me back next year. I'm sorry I didn't have time to see the gardens."

He walked her to her car and held the door open for her. "Actually, Karen, I was wondering if you'd like to stay for another couple of weeks. One weekend wasn't nearly enough time to spend with you, and I'd like to get to know you better. We'd have enough time to see the entire estate."

Perfect. "I'd love to. I must confess, I didn't really want to leave."

He swooped her into his arms. "Wonderful." His eyes gleamed with excitement and something else. Karen felt like a mouse caught in the hypnotic gaze of a snake, and she forced herself not to shiver.

She pulled away, trying to tactfully disengage herself from his embrace. "I have to go home to get some more things. I can be back tomorrow night, if that's okay."

"Of course." He opened her car door. "I miss you already."

****

Karen threw a couple more sweaters on the bed. The air was growing colder as November hovered on the horizon. "I'm going back, Misty."

Misty sat at Karen's desk flipping a pencil. "To two men who both say the other is dangerous. Sounds like a lose-lose situation to me. So how long you planning on being there?"

Karen shrugged. "Until I find out what's going on." She began folding the clothes she'd heaped on the bed and placing them in her suitcase.

Misty frowned as she watched Karen fill her bag. "It's a real education watching you pack. Everything is perfectly folded and fits exactly how you want it."

Karen shook her head. "It's just a habit I got into when I traveled with Father. The outward expression must reflect the inner peace."

"Whatever." Misty swiveled in the chair. "So, you've had some time to think. Is Randall making you forget about you know who?"

Karen realized she hadn't thought about the guy who dumped her for a while as Randall's face formed in her mind's eye. She saw Randall shirtless as he chopped wood, soaked to the skin from an October downpour, that thought dissolving into one of his striped back the last time she'd seen him.

She grabbed her suitcase. "Maybe. I don't know." She walked down the main staircase, heading straight for the front door.

Misty leaned over the railing. "I bet you dollars to doughnuts you end up with Randall before the week is out."

Karen turned around and stared at her friend. "You can't know that."

"Sure I can. You've got 'smitten' written all over your face." Misty ran down the steps. "Are you sure going back is the right thing to do?"

"Yes." She turned away, closing her eyes. "My instincts tell me this is more important than anything I've ever done before. I have to go."

Misty rolled her eyes. "After what I went through with Jack and his problems, believe me, I understand. If you need us..."

"I'll call." Karen drew an X over her heart. "Promise." She grabbed her bags, threw them in the back of her car and was off to find the answers she wanted.

****

Karen pulled up to the front door of Bradford's estate. "At least it's not raining this time," she muttered. She grabbed her bags from the back seat and climbed the few steps to the porch. The door opened and once again, the butler stood there.

I swear this guy has got to be a psionic, she thought. "Hi, again. You look a lot better, Jeffries. Bradford told me you were in the theater." She noticed his hair was still thin, but more dark gray than white. His face was full, not sunken, and his skin, though a little pale, wasn't dead white. "You're really good with makeup."

"Thank you, Ms. Spraiker," he said, giving her a small bow. "Mr. Troyington would like you to join him in the dining room. Dinner has just been served."

"Thank you." She wondered how he'd made his

voice sound so hollow before. It was deeper than she would've believed coming from such a thin man.

He gestured to an area behind the door near the wall. "You may leave your bags here. They'll be taken to your room. Mr. Troyington has put you in the same room you occupied this weekend."

"That's fine." Karen placed her bags on the floor and walked to the dining room. "Good evening."

Bradford jumped from his chair and hurried to her, grabbing her in a tight embrace. "I was hoping you'd get here for dinner." He put his arm around her waist to lead her to the table. "Edna is also staying for some extra time. She wants to get to know you, too." He leaned in to whisper, "I think she wants us to be a couple."

Karen cringed as his hand encircled her. *Why can't he keep his hands to himself?* She laughed, not wanting to give a hint of her true thoughts. "She said as much over the weekend. I like Edna. She's fun."

"She enjoys playing matchmaker. She's been trying to get me married off for years." Bradford smiled at her. "Maybe this time she'll succeed."

"You never know what the future will bring." Would she want to be Mrs. Bradford Troyington? It didn't send thrills racing through her. Why? Because every time she tried to picture Bradford, all she could see was Randall.

"Karen," Edna called. She got up, hugging Karen. "It's so nice you decided to come stay with us for a bit."

"I wanted to get to know Bradford better," she said, sitting at his left as she'd done all weekend.

Edna nodded, smiling her big secret smile at the

two of them.

"You get that look right off your face," Bradford scolded.

She shook her finger in front of his nose. "I don't have a look. I just know a good match when I see one."

Karen smiled, sipping her wine. The two certainly bantered like old friends, but she didn't feel completely at ease at the table. *What's wrong with me?* she wondered. *I can talk to a voice in a tree like we're buddies and sitting here with normal people disquiets me. This is not the way to be calm and focused. Father would be upset.*

****

Karen opened the door to the balcony and walked to the rail. She inhaled deeply, the crisp October air filling her lungs and invigorating her. She had been waiting for this moment all evening. "Are you there?" she whispered, peering into the tree.

"I'm here."

Karen breathed a sigh a relief, the tightness leaving her shoulders at the sound of his voice. "I was worried you'd think I'd left you. I'm glad you've come to see me."

"Why did you return?" he demanded. "You were out. You were safe. Why would you come back here?"

Her eyes widened in surprise at the tone of his voice. "I promised to help, remember? And I also missed..." She stopped, clamping her teeth down on her lip. It was so hard not to mention Randall at every opportunity.

Her confession diffused his anger. "You missed Randall." The voice sounded amused. "You're enamored of him even though the two of you are still strangers."

She braced her hands on the railing, leaning over as far as she could. "If you laugh at me, I swear I'll jump into that tree and kick your mystical butt."

He chuckled. "An interesting thought. And in the light from your room, I can tell your cheeks are pink."

Why did she blush every time Randall's name came up? What was wrong with her lately? Controlling her emotions was becoming a huge challenge. "I wanted to talk to you again. You're the only person I can get straight answers from."

"What questions do you want answered?"

Karen brought a chair out and placed it near the railing. "Is there such a thing as love at first sight?"

Silence fell, stretching into long seconds before he answered. "The first question you ask is one of the hardest and yet, also one of the easiest. Many people say they believe in love at first sight but don't. For a lot of people, it does happen. But I think you're looking for what should be termed as true love. True love, contrary to what people say, is a rare occurrence. Often, all it takes is one look."

Karen crossed her arms, laying her head on them as they rested on the railing. "I've never really believed in love at first sight, though I do admit it could probably happen. I mean, I haven't felt the same since Randall first looked in my car Friday night. Could something this powerful be between us? And so soon? It's like a fairy tale."

He settled on a branch. "Fairy tales have more truth than people realize. For my people, love's first kiss is the strongest act between two lovers. It can't be wasted because it can never be reclaimed. Kissing others doesn't really count. The power of true love only resonates with your soul mate."

"Really?" She paused and thought about that for a moment. "Is that why the big kiss always comes at the end of the story instead at the beginning or in the middle?"

"Yes. A couple must get to know each other and start binding their souls. You must give the power of true love as much time as possible for it to truly be able to work its magic."

Karen remembered the look in Randall's eyes when they spoke for those few precious moments as he'd been chopping wood. "Is Randall one of your people?"

"Randall and I are more than just acquaintances." He paused. "We're brothers. So, yes, that makes him part of the fairy realm." Leaves rustled as he moved closer.

She turned her head to his voice, trying to make him out. "When he said my name, I went all gushy. Why?"

"You've heard the tale of Rumpelstiltskin?" When she nodded, he continued, "That story was told to demonstrate the power of names. By saying your name, Randall has begun binding himself to you. He feels the pull between the two of you. As you've said his name more often, you've already started tying yourself to him."

"Is Randall my soul mate?" Goose bumps ran up and down her arms at the thought. Thinking of the two of them together had her blushing again.

"We believe so, yes." Again he paused. "If Troyington finds out, he won't hesitate to kill you both."

Karen shook her head. "Bradford might be harsh, but murder? That's kind of hard to believe." She sat back, rubbing her eyes. "This really is like a fairy tale. There's true love, a totally hot guy, and a villain." She turned her gaze skyward. "Where's the evil curse to do us in?"

"I fear that is still ahead of you." He sounded worried.

"It's a good thing I've got abilities of my own," she mumbled.

His voice was farther away. "What kind of abilities?"

"I have skills in martial arts combat." She chewed her lip. "There's more, but I don't know how you'll take it."

He chuckled. "I'm a creature from the fairy world in contemporary upstate New York. There's nothing you can me tell I can't believe."

She took a deep breath, then rushed her words before she could change her mind. "I'm part of a paranormal team. We all have powers and unique abilities. I have lightning reflexes. I can deflect almost anything thrown at me and send them back at my attacker. I have regeneration. I can also bend peoples' perceptions so they can't see me."

"If you are this extraordinary, what are your friends like?" He sounded impressed.

"One's a telepath, one can go intangible, one's from another dimension, one isn't even human, one can change her shape into any natural animal on earth, and our team leader was genetically constructed from a DNA sample." She paused. "We're a pretty varied group."

"This is an important secret you trust me with," he said quietly.

"I feel in my gut I can trust you. Our telepath says we've got instincts for a reason. Use them." Karen got up to sit on the rail, wanting to be closer to him. "Your turn. You got any secrets? I promise I can keep them."

She could sense him moving to the end of the branch. "I know." He was quiet, then a large hand reached out to her from the leaves. Her eyes widened, and she involuntarily stumbled away from him. Her back hit the house, and she stopped, staring at the hand. She stepped back to the rail and hesitantly touched a finger to his palm.

His hand dwarfed hers. His skin was purple and felt like rock, but still had some pliancy to it. His fingers looked longer due to the claws that curled from their ends. From the size of his hand and what she could see of his arm, she knew he had to top at least seven feet. "What are you?" she whispered.

"To some, a creature of dreams, to others, a nightmare come true." He started to pull his hand away, but Karen held it. "I don't frighten you?"

"No. Startled maybe, but not frightened." She caressed the back of his hand, smiling when she heard him sigh. "Does Bradford know about you?"

"Yes, and he's not happy about my presence here. He tries to keep me contained at night, but he and his men are finding out it's easier said than done." He squeezed her hand. "You know why Randall is treated the way he is, don't you?"

She continued to hold his hand. "Bradford has the children, doesn't he?" she said quietly.

"Exactly. To keep me in line, Randall can't show any signs of resisting Troyington or his men. If he does, the children will suffer. Troyington has made that point clear on several occasions. Every night, I come up with new ways to escape whatever cell he tries to put me in."

"But why?" Karen asked. "I don't understand why he'd take children. What does he want with them?"

"They aren't human. They're werewolf." He tightened his grip on her hand. "I'm their guardian. I'm a gargoyle. My body is closer to human than those disfigured things on the sides of churches. My race are protectors. These children were taken from the northeast pack. Guardians from across the country were sent here to find them."

"Where are they?" she asked. "I haven't seen any more like you. Are the rest of the guardians nearby?"

"Yes. Once I was established here, the rest pulled back to await further instructions. I told them their clan had lost enough. I thought I'd be able to handle what was going on, but I was overconfident. Troyington holds all the cards for now. After I find the children, I'll call them in, and we'll conclude this situation to the satisfaction of all."

That sounded more than slightly ominous. "What could Bradford want with werewolf children?"

"Troyington wants to become a shape-shifter to acquire more power in the business world. He needs their abilities. He could only get the children. Taking on adult werewolves is beyond even his men's powers."

She squeezed his hand. "Let me help," she said. "I've told you what I can do. I've got another advantage, too. Bradford likes me. I can get close to him and try to get you some information."

He held her hand tighter, giving emphasis to his words. "I don't want you putting yourself in danger. But anything you can learn, I would be grateful to hear."

Karen grinned at him. "Please. I've fought some of the most powerful supervillains on the planet. I can handle this crowd. I'd better go inside." She stood, slowly pulling her hand from his. "Bradford wants to show me around tomorrow. Good night, Guardian."

"Good night, Karen."

Her insides turned to jelly just as they had when Randall said her name. She stumbled across the threshold to her room. She flung herself on her bed, turning over to stare at the ceiling.

"This gets worse all the time," she mumbled. "I've got one guy who wants to hook up with me, one guy who makes me think indecent things, and a voice that belongs to a gargoyle and gives me goose bumps." Her grip on her emotions was slipping more and more the longer she was here. She put a pillow over her face and screamed.

Chapter Six

"I believe I promised you a tour of the gardens," Bradford said at breakfast.

Karen nodded. "Yes, you did. I can't wait to see them." She cringed inwardly as she covered his hand with hers. After finding out Bradford had kidnapped children and was planning on hurting them or worse, she wanted no contact with him at all. But she had to keep up appearances so he wouldn't suspect what she knew. "Is it a four season garden?"

"I think so. I'm not good with flowers. All I know is my gardener keeps them full and eye-catching all year long," he said. "I never see any blossoms in the winter, but I believe he put in some type of fancy grasses to keep it looking fresh even when it snows."

"I can't wait to see them." *At least that much is true*, she thought. She loved gardens and all kinds of flowers even though she personally never had any luck with them. Her father tended the gardens at Angel Haven. He always said she didn't need luck with flowers, just patience, tenderness, and a whole lot of knowledge.

They left through the same french doors they had before, heading off to their right. Karen gasped when she saw the gardens. A low brick wall surrounded the flowers that waved merrily in the bright sunshine. Red, gold, pink, purple, and blue all meshed together, their colors planted in harmony to each other and the area around them.

"I've never seen anything like this," Karen said. "Your gardener does good work. Everything blends so well, it's hard to tell where one section ends and another begins." She leaned down to smell some of the blooms they were passing.

A narrow, gray flagstone path wound its way through the bright blossoms. Bradford put his arm around her waist when they'd entered, stopping here and there so she could see everything, finally pausing to sit on a white stone bench, near a gurgling fountain. He scowled when he saw Cray approaching them.

"Morning, Ms. Spraiker," he said with a nod in Karen's direction. "Mr. Troyington, we have a problem at the stables. Harmon says he needs you down there immediately."

"You have stables?" Karen asked. "I'd love to see them."

Cray gave a slight shake of his head.

"Maybe you should stay here," Bradford said, never taking his eyes from Cray. "I'm not sure what's going on, and it might not be pretty."

"Maybe I can help." Karen didn't want to be left behind. Going with Bradford might help her understand what was going on at the mansion.

"This isn't a good time, ma'am," Cray said.

Bradford turned to her, concern in his eyes as he took her hand. "Are you sure?"

"I'm sure." She smiled at Bradford, trying to convince him to take her. She wasn't going to get any answers if she couldn't find out anything from the rest of his people.

He nodded at her and squeezed her hand. "All right. Let's go see what the trouble is."

The three of them strode down a slight hill to the stables. Harmon had Randall's arm twisted behind his back, his thick arm wrapped around Randall's neck. Randall was covered with dust, and the stable master was sporting a bleeding lip and a black eye.

"Harmon," Bradford barked. "What're you doing?"

"I've told this freak to stay away from my animals," Harmon ground out. "Now he's going to learn the hard way I mean what I say."

"Let him go." Bradford demanded. "*Now*."

Harmon shoved Randall away from him. "Stay out of my stables or the next time you won't walk away. Understood?"

Randall glared at him, the tenseness in his arms belying the calm posture he adopted. He stepped toward Harmon, his right arm lifting a little as his hand balled.

Bradford shoved Randall toward the door. "Get outside." He turned to Karen. "This will only take a moment." He motioned Cray to follow him.

After Bradford left, Karen approached Harmon. "Do you take care of all the animals here?" she asked, gesturing at the twenty full stalls.

"Yes. Only five belong to Mr. Troyington. The rest are all boarded here for his neighbors." His eyes narrowed as he watched her go to the first horse and stroke its nose.

"You do a great job. They all look in fine health." Karen didn't dare take her eyes from the horse. She knew she'd try to look outside to see what was happening with Randall and then they'd both be in trouble.

Harmon's posture relaxed a little. "They're like my children. Mr. Troyington says I like them more than people."

"I guess you don't like the others interfering out here," she said, turning to watch him closely.

He scowled. "No, I don't. And I really don't like Dupré being out here. He upsets my animals."

Why? she thought. *How does he upset them?* "Would it be all right, if when you're here, I can come see them?" Karen asked. She petted the horse, feeling Harmon's gaze penetrating her.

Apparently satisfied by his scrutiny, he said, "Yes, but only when I'm here."

Bradford came in. "Everything's all sorted out. Ready to continue our walk?" They headed outside, continuing on the same route they'd been on earlier.

Karen linked her arm through his. "Absolutely. Mr. Harmon said I can come down to see the horses, but only when he's there."

"He must trust you." He sounded impressed. "Harmon lets no one near his children unless he has to."

They walked the grounds around the house. Jeffries stood on the drawing room porch as they drew closer. "Mr. Troyington, you have a business call."

He turned an apologetic smile to her. "Would you excuse me again? I'm sure this won't take long." He kissed the back of her hand.

"Sure. I'll wait for you out here." She breathed a mental sigh of relief. A few minutes to herself was just what she needed to collect her thoughts.

She resisted the urge to wipe her hand on her pants after he kissed it, smiling at him instead. After he'd gone, she heard angry voices coming from the side of the house. She crept forward, calling on her ability to hide herself from view. Cray stomped away, and she peered around the corner to see Randall enter the wood shed. She dropped her invisibility and darted inside.

She stopped short when she saw him. Randall leaned against the wall, the back of his shirt torn. She walked over to him and moved the fabric aside, her eyes widening when there was nothing there, just smooth, unblemished skin.

"You're completely healed," she whispered.

"I'm a fast healer." He smiled at her. His eyes crinkled at the corners, giving him an impish look.

Karen's knees went wobbly. "Why do you let them do this to you?" she asked softly.

"I thought our friend explained it to you," he said, pain coloring his words. "Any sign of defiance on my part and the children will suffer." He winced and rubbed his side. "Until the guardian's charges are found, I'm stuck with Troyington's abuse."

Karen crossed to him, laying her hand on his shoulder. She tried to ignore the hardness of his muscles, the heat that radiated from him. She swallowed audibly. She forced herself not to start kneading that shoulder, to relieve the tenseness she found there. She moved closer to him.

"What—" She cleared her throat, trying to make her voice not quite so shaky. "What can I do to help you?"

He straightened and took a small step nearer to her. "Keep Troyington happy. Do that and he'll stay out of my way."

Karen's mouth went dry. She hesitated before raising her hand to his jaw. She just stood there, staring at him, memorizing every line of his face.

He captured her hand, placing it over his heart. "I know what the guardian told you about true love."

"Do you think he's right?" she whispered. "Could we be soul mates?"

"Anything's possible."

She gazed at him. Even if she didn't know about his ties to the fairy realm, she would've thought him magical. The wild blue-black hair, the hardness and perfection of his body, and those blue eyes that held a hint of something otherworldly. He smiled at her again, as if guessing her thoughts. She ran her hand over the planes of his chest and down his arm. He was always so warm, like he generated his own heat.

What would happen, she thought, *if I kissed him, right here, right now? I know what the guardian said, but no man has the right to look this tempting. Somebody, anybody, give me strength.*

Before her thoughts ran away with her, she asked, "What will we do when this is over?"

"Whatever's necessary." He looked out the door. "You'd better get back. He'll be looking for you."

Karen nodded, not trusting her weak voice any longer. Before she could stop herself, she wrapped her arms around him, holding him tight. She closed her eyes, savoring the feel of him in her arms. "Please be safe."

He pressed his cheek to the top of her head, his arms wrapping tightly around her waist. "They haven't stopped me yet. Now, go."

Karen could feel her body tremble and awaken at his touch. The world felt alive when she was with him and she knew in that instant that he held her, she wanted him with as intensity that was building the longer he held her. She didn't want to let him go and sensed he felt the same. She forced herself to step back. "Will I see you soon?"

"Of course. We're on the same property." He grinned at her. "I'll try to talk to you again."

He laid his hand on her cheek and moved a little closer to her. "You make me want to break all the rules I'm bound to," he whispered. "I can't wait for this to be over."

"Me, too," she said. She leaned into his caress, wishing he could do more as her body began aching for him in rather intimate places. She finally pulled away and held on to the wall for a minute to make her knees stop quivering. She stumbled out the door, turning to get another look at him.

A blackbird sitting on the roof of the shed grabbed her attention. Its call seemed to laugh at her, mocking her. It stared directly at her for a few more seconds before taking flight. She watched it go, then ran back to where Bradford had left her, taking great gulps of air to try to steady herself as the french doors opened.

Bradford came out, smiling. "That was tedious. I hate to tell you this, but I have to go to New York City tomorrow and deal with a company crisis. Do you want to come with me?"

"I think I'll stay here. It'll give me and Edna a chance to have a girls' day." Karen leaned into him. "And I'd like to explore the woods. Would you mind?"

"Not a bit." They headed back toward the gardens. "The woods have identifiable trails. The teachers from the town bring the children here for nature walks. As long as you stay on the marked paths, you should be fine." He paused. "Will the two of you be all right?"

"Sure," she said. "We've got a whole house full of servants to help us. We'll be fine." *And I've got a guardian and a sexy, southern man. I'll be A-okay.*

****

"What has happened today to make you smile so?" the guardian asked when he arrived. He came closer to the balcony, part of his body visible through the foliage.

She could feel the familiar burning on her cheeks as she remembered her day. "I got to see some horses," she stammered.

"Is that all?" His tone indicated he knew more of her day.

"I talked to Randall today." She stopped and chewed her lip. How much more should she say?

"You can tell me anything, remember?" He reached out from the shadows to take her hand. "Randall has already told me a bit of what happened in the wood shed."

Her grip on his hand tightened. "He makes me feel—I don't know, it's indescribable." She frowned, searching for the right words. "It's like I'm hot and cold and then nervous, then not and then, *kablooey*, I explode."

The guardian actually laughed, his voice sounding like rocks falling down a cliff. "I know exactly what you mean. You've just described the feelings of true love."

"That wasn't a very good description. But he makes me feel so..." she paused, "emotional." She stared at his hand, trying to make sense of everything she said and felt. Not going to happen, she thought. "I don't like losing control of my emotions."

"It's okay to give in to a little lost control occasionally. Would it make you feel better to know you do the same to him?" He still sounded amused.

"Really?" Karen thought about that for a minute. It was comforting to know he felt the same things she did. "Then you and I were right when we talked last and Randall and I are supposed to be together."

"I would say that's a reasonable assumption," he agreed, giving her hand a squeeze.

"I feel like we're being watched, though, and not just by human eyes. This is getting way out of control." She thought about the bird on the shed. It really had felt like it was watching her. "Tomorrow, Bradford's going to the city on business. I'm hoping I can talk to Randall again without his goons busting in."

He squeezed her hand. "Troyington's eyes are everywhere. Randall is rarely left alone. I've already told you what will happen if Troyington finds out."

"I know. But I can't turn my back on you guys when you're trying to save children." She sighed. "I don't remember fairy tales being this complicated."

"You don't know the ones I know."

Karen looked at the hand holding hers. "Does Randall know you're putting the moves on me?"

He laughed again. "Yes. We have no secrets. He says I don't have a chance. I knew this." His voice turned serious. "You've already lost your heart. No man but your soul mate has a chance to win you."

Karen laid her forehead on his hand, thankful for the rocky coolness of his skin. "I'm glad you know what's going on. Today when he smiled at me, I was tempted to throw him down right there. I could feel how much he wanted to kiss me, and I know I wanted to kiss him." She raised her head. "But I remembered what you said about love's first kiss. I don't want to jump the gun or anything, but something needs to happen soon before I go crazy."

He tightened his grip on her hand. "Be strong a little longer. I may have a lead on where the children are. They're being moved to somewhere on the estate. If he's bringing them closer, he and his scientist, Dr. Strathmore, have had a breakthrough."

Karen sat up straighter. "I'll walk around the estate tomorrow and see if I can find anything."

"Please be careful."

She grinned. "Always. Besides, these guys around here couldn't catch me even if they tried." She stood, pulling her hand from him. "I'd better get some rest." She paused at the door to her room. She looked at the tree where he hid himself. "When do I get to see the rest of you?"

"When the time is right and not before."

She sighed and shook her head. "I forgot that annoying quality of fairy tales. You get a lot of cryptic answers. Good night, Guardian."

"Good night, Karen."

She stopped before going in and watched as a huge silhouette sprung from the top of the tree, the wings stretching out to blend with the darkness.

Chapter Seven

Karen wandered the grounds after an early breakfast, the sun barely topping the trees around the estate. Bradford had left before she got downstairs, and Edna was nowhere to be found. He'd been insistent she stay on the trails in the woods. She smiled. The more interesting things were usually found off the beaten path.

I hope Cray and Harmon are busy elsewhere today.

Leaves and twigs crunched under her feet as the trees closed in around her. Sunlight poked holes through the colorful canopy over her head, and birds chirped to each other. She heard crackling and saw a squirrel sitting on a branch eating something it held in its tiny paws. She sighed and wished her thoughts were as peaceful as the area around her. She slowed her steps as voices drifted her way.

Her heart pounded against her ribs as Randall's voice reached her. "What else did the water nixies say?"

A light female voice, reminding Karen of wind through trees, answered, "They caught a glimpse of them further downstream. They couldn't follow them any further because they went more inland."

He snorted. "I'm surprised they followed them as far as they did. What about the brownies? Have they seen anything?"

"They found a small cabin up in the hills. They say work has been done on it." Karen crept up behind a large tree and leaned around to watch them. Randall looked so serious and a small woman paced in front of him.

He rubbed his chin. "It's got to be where they're moving the kids to. Ask the wood folk to keep watch on it."

The woman with Randall couldn't have been more than three feet tall. Her skin was light tan, her spring green hair resembled leaves falling down her back, and her arms were thin. Karen couldn't see the rest of her because she was dressed like the goth teenagers at the mall. She wore large pants that covered her feet and a tight black T-shirt with a pink skull emblazoned across the front. Black studded bands encircled both wrists, matching the choker around her neck.

The change in Randall was amazing. His voice had lost that hard edge she'd heard when he spoke about Bradford or his men. His body was more relaxed and a heck of a lot more desirable. Karen wished he could be like this all the time, but knew until his mission was complete, there was no hope of that happening. She watched him a few more minutes then stepped out from her hiding place. "Randall?"

The small woman's head swung around. She gestured to the trees near Karen, speaking a word in a strange language. Vines snapped to life as leaves flung themselves at Karen's face, their brittle stems stinging her skin. She dodged the first few vines, but more shot her way, ensnaring her wrists and ankles. She pulled against them, but the more she fought, the tighter they became.

"Hey, cut it out!" she shouted.

"It's all right, Raesheen," Randall said. "Cut her loose."

The woman glared at Karen. "Are you sure? She could be one of Troyington's spies."

Randall smiled, placing his hand on her shoulder. "She isn't. Trust me." He headed for Karen.

The woman scrutinized him, then shrugged. "Suit yourself." At her command, the vines released Karen, letting her fall to the ground in an undignified heap.

She rubbed her backside as Randall pulled her to her feet. "What just happened?"

"My friend. Come on, I'll introduce you." He walked her back to where the woman waited. "Raesheen, this is Karen. Karen, this is Raesheen. She's a dryad."

"That explains the plant attack," Karen said with a smile. "It's very nice to meet you." She stuck out her hand.

Raesheen eyed her warily, then grabbed Karen's hand in a strong grip. "She's the one we sensed?"

He nodded. "Yes, and be nice. She's believed in us all her life."

She narrowed her eyes, staring intently at Karen. "I can't feel any evil in her, nor can I pick up any hidden agendas. I believe she's here to help us." The dryad stood back. "I approve."

Randall smiled at his friend. "Glad to hear it."

The dryad walked around her and studied her more intently. "The Oracle certainly knows what she's talking about. The dragon spirit is the very essence of her strength."

"I know," he agreed. "It pulls you in with its power. I didn't think humans had that kind of ability in them."

"Would you two quit talking about me like I'm not even here?" Karen interrupted.

"Sorry," Randall said. "We may have more information on the children."

"That's great," Karen said, thinking how normal it felt to be standing in the middle of the woods with a dryad and a breathtakingly handsome man, talking about kidnapped werewolf children. "Where do you think they might be headed?"

"A small cabin in the hills," Randall said. "The wood folk say Troyington rents it to hunters."

Raesheen lifted her head, listening to the wind. "I have to go. I'm being called by the Court. I'll be in touch." She laid her hand on Randall's arm. "Be careful, my friend." Staring at Karen, she said, "Be well. Keep yourself safe." Walking to a tree, she disappeared inside it.

Karen stared after her for a moment. "She doesn't look like any dryad I've seen in books. I didn't think dryads were into the goth look. And was she wearing combat boots?"

He nodded. Taking her arm, he led her back to the path. "She decided to modernize herself when her mother, the queen, retired and moved to Tahiti. The rest of her subjects followed her lead. Most fairies these days don't dress in traditional clothes any more. Raesheen developed a taste for the goth style. A lot of the wood folk wear jeans and work clothes. Most of them carry cell phones, and you don't know gaming addiction until you see a gnome with a video game."

Randall grinned at her. "We're people, just like humans."

There went those wobbly knees again. She cleared her throat. "People that humans think don't exist," she said. "She's queen of the fairies? How long have you known her?"

He drifted closer to Karen as they walked. "You wouldn't believe me if I told you. And she doesn't rule everything, just our piece of it down south. Her mother was queen of the southern realm. Raesheen and I grew up together in Louisiana, and when I was called north, she came with me."

Karen's brows drew down as she tried to make sense of what he'd said. "This doesn't sound like any of the tales I read when I was little. According to the stories, fairies didn't always get along."

He shrugged. "Fairy courts are usually very territorial, but everyone is up in arms about the werewolf children. We both have permission to be here from the clans that rule this part of the country." He frowned. "There'd been several rescue attempts before I got here. Troyington thought at first they were just human, but Harmon found out from the animals who they really were. Troyington knew who I was the minute I arrived and knew I had powers of my own, so he kept me alive, but on a tight leash. I work around the estate, usually under Cray's supervision. Sometimes, I'm lucky enough to slip away."

Karen's arm brushed his and she jumped. His touch constantly sent shockwaves through her body. Now, with all she'd learned about Bradford and Randall, things were getting more complicated all the time. "How could Bradford kill creatures of magic?"

He stared straight ahead. "We all have our weaknesses. Turns out, he found ours. Harmon compelled the animals to tell him. The people that work for him have abilities, like you. I figured it had to be someone with power to take on the northeast werewolf pack and get away with it."

She watched his eyes darken with checked anger and sadness over what had been done to his brethren. Power rolled off him in waves and her own answered strongly, making her shiver. *Oh, Bradford, you've really opened a big can of worms.*

"Troyington made me sign a contract stating I wouldn't harm him or his people." He winked at her, and the disarming grin was back. "I snuck in my own clause when I signed. It says if it's in the children's best interest, I can do whatever I think necessary to whoever I want."

A headache began behind her eyes. She rubbed the back of her neck. *I don't think I can take in too much more information.* "Why can't you just do what you need to find the children?"

He stopped, turning her to him. "When any magic creature signs a contract or makes a promise, they're bound by it to uphold it to the best of their abilities. I have no choice. I'm bound by the contract I signed. That's why I amended it before putting my signature on it. If they do anything to the kids, I can take matters into my own hands in the pack's best interest."

Karen laid her hand on his arm, savoring the feel of his skin under her fingers. Again, her power flared at the contact, and she was ready to jump him right then and there. She saw light glow in his eyes briefly as he watched her. "Harmon said you upset his animals.

How? I thought animals and the fairy world got along."

"We do. I was talking to the horses to find out what they'd seen." He shrugged. "He walked in when I was getting answers. He saw it as they were upset. I saw it as finally getting an intelligent answer."

"You talk to animals too? Why am I not surprised?" They continued walking back to the mansion, Karen shivering in the chill morning air. "Why aren't you ever cold?" He still wore no jacket outside.

He shrugged. "I'm not affected by the weather as much as humans."

Karen watched him glance at her, and she smiled just a little. "I'm still having a hard time believing you're not human." She ran her hand down his arm. He felt as warm as if he'd been in the summer sun for hours. "You feel human." *Really, really human.* Her face grew hot as she stared at him.

He cocked an eyebrow, the look on his face saying he suspected what was going through her mind. "I'm half human. My mother's human. My father's a guardian, like our mutual friend."

She searched his face. "He said you have feelings for me." She stared into the depths of those magical eyes. "Do you?" She could almost feel what he kept protected in his heart. Knowing more about him, she could see the inhuman part of him, the wildness she had sensed, dance in those blue, blue eyes.

He brushed his knuckles over her cheek. "Yes," he admitted. "I do."

She closed her eyes and held his hand to her face. She stepped closer to him. "We can be together, right? I mean, your parents are together."

"Yes. She gave up everything to be with him. She understood how important the guardians are to the fairy world." He leaned down and whispered, "Could you give up everything for me?"

"Right now, yes, I could." Her chest heaved as she tried to catch her breath.

He leaned a little closer, dropping his hand to the side of her neck, then to her collar bone. "But it wouldn't be for just now. It would be forever." His finger traced a line down to the top button of her shirt.

Karen ran her hands along his chest and up to his face. The warmth of his skin flowed into her hands, filling her whole body. He leaned closer as she caressed his face.

"Dupré!"

Cray's shout shattered the stillness, ruining the moment. Randall stepped back, smiling as Karen's cheeks burned. "We'd better get back. We don't want Troyington's men to find us out here."

"No." Disappointment swept through her. But didn't this kind of stuff always happen in fairy tales? The path to true love was always filled with obstacles. *Yes*, she thought. *But why does my path have major construction signs?*

"Go back the way you came." He nodded off to his right. "There's a shortcut down that way I can take to come out at another area on the estate."

She wrapped her arms around him. "Promise me you'll be careful." She gazed at his face, searching for the magic they'd shared moments before. She held him tighter when he smiled, turning her legs to jelly. *If he doesn't quit that, I'll be helping him from a jar.*

He gazed in her eyes. "Everything will be fine.

Trust me."

"Dupré!" The shout was much closer this time.

Randall ran down the path and in moments had disappeared. Karen resumed her leisurely stroll, drifting out of the woods not ten feet from Cray. "Good morning, Mr. Cray. Was that you shouting just now?"

"Yes, ma'am. I'm looking for Dupré. Have you seen him?" Cray glanced over her shoulder, searching for Randall.

"No. I was taking a walk. Mr. Troyington said I should stay on the path. I'm waiting for Edna." She smiled what she hoped was an innocent smile. "If I see him, should I tell him you're looking for him?"

"If you wouldn't mind." Cray stomped off toward the mansion.

Karen sagged against a tree, breathing a sigh a relief. A squirrel sat near her feet, staring at her. Again, a blackbird's mocking call echoed around her. Making her way back to the house, she had a strange feeling that the animals were spying on her. A dull ache started in her temple, and she rubbed her head.

****

"Edna, good morning," Karen called. *I'll bet your morning wasn't nearly as exciting as mine.* Her face grew warm, still feeling Randall's light touch. If she put his impish grin with it, she may as well confess every feeling he crammed into her body.

Edna slammed the door shut she'd just come out of. "Good morning, dear. Did you sleep well?"

"Yes, thank you." She nodded at the door behind the older woman. "What's that room?"

Edna looked over her shoulder at the door she'd just locked. "This is Bradford's private study. He does all his important work in there. I help him sometimes."

Did Edna seem a little nervous? Karen mentally shrugged. It was probably her own close call with the handyman outside coloring her perceptions. "Oh. Do you think he'd show it to me sometime?"

"I'm not sure," Edna said slowly. "He's particular about who goes in there. I think I'm lucky I get to go in." She smiled at Karen, taking her arm and leading her away. "Oh, let him have his secrets. What shall we do today?"

Karen had her own plan in place. "I was hoping you could show me around. I'm sure I haven't seen half of this place yet, and I didn't want to wander around by myself, just in case there were places, like this room, I wasn't supposed to go in."

"That's a wonderful idea." Edna winked at her. "Then you'll see I know what I'm talking about when I tell you Bradford is right for you." They stood in the hall while Edna thought. "Let's start on this floor. We've already been through the basement pretty thoroughly."

She took Karen into the library. Karen inhaled the scent of the leather-bound tomes lining the tall shelves. French doors opened into the garden and the curtains were drawn back to let the morning sun light up the room. "Do you think it would be all right if I borrowed a book while I'm here? I forgot to bring my own with me."

"I don't think Bradford would have a problem with it. I think there's very little he'd deny you." Edna peered closely at her. "You've been staying away from that Dupré fellow, haven't you?"

"Of course." Did her feelings for him show on her

face? "I realized everyone here knows him much better than I do." *But that's slowly changing*, she thought.

Bradford's regular study was sparsely furnished compared to what she'd seen of the rest of the house so far. Just a desk and a few filing cabinets with a small stereo on a table by the wall. Next door was the billiard room, which led to the ballroom. The air felt stale and unused. "Does he use these rooms much?"

"Not really." Edna gestured around the room. "He added them because he found out his neighbors had them. He didn't want them thinking he couldn't keep up."

That fit with what Karen was finding out about the millionaire so far. He wanted things others had and planned to get them. The fact that he took werewolf children in order to claim their abilities spoke volumes about his character. Adding on a couple of rooms to keep up with his neighbors was nothing to him. How much time did Randall and the children have left before Troyington got impatient with not being able to do the things they could? The dull throb in her temple intensified.

Karen went on with the tour, trying to ignore the incessant pounding in her head. This might be the only chance she'd have to look around without Bradford being there. All her body wanted was to lie down. Preferably with Randall. She gave a mental sigh, wishing her mind would quit sneaking in those totally distracting comments.

The kitchen turned out to be much smaller than she expected. "I would've thought the kitchen would be huge with an army of cooks."

Edna chuckled. "No, he's only got one cook. He

had the kitchen redesigned to her specifications. She told him she didn't need something the size of a barn to fix meals in. This suits her just fine. And it's just her, no one else. She's very possessive of the kitchen." Edna opened a door in the far corner. "Let's go upstairs and I'll show you the other bedrooms."

She led Karen up the back stairs, and they came out at the end of the hallway. Most of the bedrooms near these stairs were closed off, curtains pulled tight and covers draped the furniture, making odd shapes in the near dark. The air felt stale and dust tickled her nose. She sneezed. "Are these rooms ever used?"

Edna pulled a small pack of tissues out of her pants pocket and handed them to her. "Very rarely. They won't be opened now until next summer. He always entertains in the summer."

They went a little further down the hall, and Edna opened the door closest to the main staircase. Karen knew instantly it was Bradford's room. It reflected the man himself, soft, yet masculine. The ivory and tan colors were light and restful, the furniture definitely for a man, but not the heavy dark things one would expect. His closet was its own room, leading to a huge private bathroom.

"All this luxury could really ruin a person," Karen said, craning her neck to see everything at once.

Edna laughed. "I'll show you my room. It's not nearly as grand as this, but it suits me." She led Karen to the door directly across from Karen's room and flung it open. "Here it is."

The room was pastel blue. Little pink flowers brightened the wallpaper, the comforter, and the matching curtains. "I have this room every time I come here."

"It's very sweet," Karen said. "Just like you."

Edna lightly slapped her wrist. "Stop. You'll have an old lady blushing in a minute."

Karen walked around the room, admiring the white antique furniture and the view from the windows. She could see the wood shed where she and Randall always seemed to meet up. Had Edna seen them together? If so, had she told Bradford?

As she turned, a sparkle of sunlight on the floor caught her eye. She stepped closer, cutting the glare and saw a medical syringe.

Why would a syringe be in Edna's room? Did she need insulin or some other medication? Was she a drug addict? Karen wasn't sure if she wanted to consider the other options. What if Edna was somehow involved with the missing werewolves? Karen's face froze into the smile she'd pasted on. The headache lanced through her temple as she tried to keep Edna from suspecting how she felt.

"Can we walk around the balcony before lunch?" she asked.

Edna looked at her watch. "I think we have time. The view of the garden from up here is wonderful." She opened the door, and they stepped into the chill air.

Karen barely heard what Edna was talking about. She was looking for Randall and wishing she could talk to him. The occupants of the grand house sent chills down her spine. She prayed silently for time to move quickly. If ever she needed to talk to the guardian, it was now.

Chapter Eight

"Thanks for an informative day," Karen said as she and Edna sat down to dinner. She'd popped enough extra-strength everything to make her head stop throbbing, getting it down to a dull, but bearable ache. The warm, amber light from the chandelier was low, making it easier to sit there.

Edna poured blood-colored wine from the decanter into their glasses. "My pleasure."

"Good evening, ladies," Bradford said from the doorway.

Karen stood. "You're back early. We missed you." *Liar*, her inner voice screamed at her, making the headache stab sharply for a second.

Edna turned in her seat to smile at him. "Yes, we did. It was too quiet without you here."

Bradford took his usual seat, the yellow-orange glow from the chandelier casting strange, dancing shadows over his face. "We wrapped things up quicker than expected." He reached out and grabbed Karen's hand. "I didn't want to spend any more time away from you. So, how did you two spend your day?"

Karen gritted her teeth, resisting the urge to snatch her hand away. She caught a glimpse of something in his eyes that made her shiver, and she looked away quickly. "Edna showed me around," she said, nodding to the older woman. "I knew the house was huge, but I had no idea there were so many rooms."

Bradford glanced at her. "Sometimes this place is a bit much for me. That's why I'm glad you stayed longer. It gets lonely here." He shrugged. "But it was my parents' home, so I can't bring myself to sell it."

"Is that why you had the murder mystery weekend even though you're busy with work right now?" she asked. "To have people around?"

"Exactly." He raised his glass to her. "You really are a good detective."

Karen stared at her plate as she pushed the food around. "Thanks."

"Maybe before you leave, I'll have a party."

"That'd be great. I'd like to meet your friends." Karen drank some wine, trying to wash the lies out of her mouth.

****

Edna left Karen and Bradford alone in the drawing room after dinner, saying she needed to call her sister.

"I think she planned this." He grinned.

Karen laughed, trying hard to conceal her nervousness. "I'm sure you're right." This was the last thing she wanted. Her confidence at being alone with Bradford wasn't very high and she felt he knew it.

He turned on the CD player, soft music filling the room. He held out his hand. "Shall we practice, just in case there's time for a get-together?"

She accepted his hand, rising to her feet. "Sure. I love dancing."

He held her close as they swayed in time to the smooth music surrounding them. She couldn't pull away without making him suspicious, so she focused her thoughts on Randall instead. How would it feel to be held by him like this? What would happen when the music stopped? She itched to pull out of Bradford's grasp, but her own feelings didn't matter. She was doing this for Randall and the kids. She needed information. Time to say something.

"I found out one of your secrets today," she whispered.

"Oh?" His voice was a smooth purr.

Karen detected no change in him. She let the statement hang a moment more, trying to make him sweat. "I found out you have a private office. Edna was coming out of it this morning. She says she helps you with your work at times."

"It's true," he said. "My private office is really nothing special. I keep everything extremely important or time sensitive in there."

She pulled away from him slightly. "Any chance I can see it sometime?" He didn't feel like Randall. He felt manufactured, fake. Randall was warm and felt like the woods she found him in, natural and untamed. *Stop it*, she told herself.

He held her tighter. "It's just dull business paperwork."

"But if it's important to you, I'd like to be part of it." The answers she wanted were probably in there.

The smile on his lips didn't reach his eyes. "Maybe someday. Now, what about you? Any private office for you?" His grip on her hand tightened as he watched her, almost studying her.

She laughed. "No. I run my own martial arts school. I have an assistant to do office stuff. I teach classes." She smiled at him. "I love the kids. It's so great when they get a particular move right."

His hand traveled up and down her back. "You certainly are full of surprises. I didn't think your career would be so physical."

She flinched, just a tiny bit. Think of the kids, she reminded herself. It's for the kids. "What did you think I did for a living?"

"Truthfully, I saw you as more of the business type." He lowered her arms and slowly slid her light jacket off her shoulders. Then he opened the top button on her shirt. "I missed you, Karen."

She stepped back. "I missed you, too." *No, you didn't*, her inner voice screamed as Bradford kissed her. *You were upset when he showed up. And right now, all you want is Randall to be kissing you instead of him.* She lowered her eyes. "I'd better go upstairs. I don't want to rush things between us."

Anger flared in his eyes so briefly, Karen almost believed she imagined it. Almost. A second later, his smile was back, but his eyes weren't as warm as before. "I understand," he said. "I'll see you tomorrow."

"Give me time," she whispered. "It'll be worth the wait."

She supposed Bradford thought his kiss would excite her, but all she wanted was her toothbrush. And he was fast with his hands. She closed the top three buttons of her shirt as she mounted the stairs. Randall's face filled her mind. She could almost feel his arms around her. Her breath quickened, and she tripped on the last few steps. Her insides flamed, making her fan herself with her hand.

She slammed the door to her room and headed straight for the balcony. She leaned on the rail, taking big gulps of the cool night air. *Will I ever get to kiss*

Randall? She was beginning to doubt it. The guardian told her the big kiss always comes at the end of the story. She wasn't even sure her story had an end, let alone a happy one. Hot tears slipped down her cheeks. "Damn," she murmured.

She could feel the calm face she always showed people beginning to slip away. Emotions rolled through her, starting her trembling all over again. She was losing control over herself and didn't know how to stop it. Worse. She didn't think she wanted to stop it.

"Good evening, Karen."

She jumped. The guardian was closer to her than ever, his voice right in her ear.

"Oh, hey." She wiped her eyes with the back of her hand. "I'm glad you're here."

"You've been crying." She could hear the frown in his voice. "Who has hurt you? They'll not do so again."

"No one," she choked out. "Just too many thoughts, not enough action."

"You've been thinking of Randall?" he asked quietly.

She turned back to the railing, staring out into the darkness. "Yes. I'm tired of quick embraces. I want to be held in a way that leads to interesting conclusions. I want to stop using my imagination." She slammed her hands on the railing. "I don't want to wait for the end of my story for a kiss."

Leaves rustled near the balcony rail. "I understand what you're going through." His voice soothed her, calming her jangled emotions. "I know it's hard, and I know it hurts. Trust us both. It's only for a little longer. Then you'll have your story's end."

Karen cursed the tears that fell again. "He said he

has feelings for me. I know I do for him. I just want us to have a moment to let us explore those feelings." If this was what Misty went through with Jack, she no longer felt jealous. True love was hard work, harder than she ever thought possible.

"How am I going to get through this?" she whispered.

His large hand came through the leaves and lightly rested on her shoulder. "Believe me when I tell you he's as frustrated as you. He feels his need as strongly as you do yours."

"Good," she pouted. "I'm glad I'm not in this alone."

The guardian laughed. "That's more like it. Be strong. The time will come sooner than you think."

She took a deep breath to steady herself. "Bradford has a private study. I'm sure there's something in there that can help you. It stays locked."

"Randall mentioned this study, also."

Maybe he would know more about Edna and the syringe she'd found on the floor. "Edna, the older woman that's staying here with him, showed me around today. When I was in her room, I found a needle. I'm not sure if she has a medical condition. She never said anything about one."

He squeezed her shoulder. "You're still safe, aren't you?"

She patted his hand. "Yes. They both think I'm warming to Bradford."

Silence. Then, "Are you?"

She looked at him with disbelief. "How can you ask that? After what I've found out about Bradford, every time he touches me, my skin crawls. Yet, I deal with it because Randall needs me to keep Bradford busy so he can look for the children." She shook her head. "We're both stuck with Bradford's unwanted attentions until the children are safe."

She walked away, folding her arms as she turned her back to him. "Then I just get done telling you Randall has all of my emotions on pins and needles and you ask if I have feelings for Bradford! Maybe I should kick your mystical butt."

He chuckled at her outrage. "He'll be glad to know about your emotional state."

"Are you done making fun of me?" She waited for an answer. Nothing. "Thank you. May I continue?"

"Please do, dear one."

She lowered her voice. "I asked Edna about a small, unused room in the basement of this place and she said that Cray uses it sometimes when he has work to do. I know I saw blood in there, and she just made light of it. When she took me on a tour of the house, I found the syringe in her room. Does she have some sort of medical condition? Has she done something to Randall?"

Karen sensed him pulling away as he withdrew his hand. "No," he told her. "She didn't do anything to him yet, and she doesn't have any medical problems we're aware of. Edna is Dr. Strathmore, one of the country's leading geneticists. She's close to Troyington. She'll tell him everything if she knows how you feel about Randall."

She chewed her bottom lip. "Is she spying on me?"

Leaves rustled near the trunk. "It's possible. She'll hurt you to protect Troyington. Keep your guard up around her. Watch what you do and say."

Karen frowned. "Her bedroom window looks over the wood shed." Her hands shook as nausea crawled through her stomach. "Could she have seen Randall and me together?"

"Possibly." Warmth crept back in his voice. "I'll tell Randall all you told me."

"Not everything," she insisted. "I mean it. Not one word about pins and needles."

****

Karen's alarm woke her as the sun began to rise. She yanked up her jeans and pulled a heavy sweater over her shirt. She hoped Randall would be at the clearing she'd seen him in yesterday. It was a long shot, but she had to try. The house was dark and silent as she slipped out the french doors, retracing her steps from the day before.

Randall stood in the clearing and her face burned as she watched him in the light of the rising sun. He was naked, the dawn bathing him in an ethereal, orange glow, turning his tanned skin deep gold. As he lifted his arms, she watched his back ripple with strength. Her eyes drifted down to the tightness in his buttocks, the power in his legs. His hair fluttered in the early morning breeze, making her want to run her hands through it, to feel his skin, to capture the very essence of who he was right now.

As he laid his head back, she glimpsed a smile of pure joy on his face as the sun rose higher. The muscles in his arms tightened and stretched as he moved them straight out and slowly lowered them to his sides. He seemed more than just a man. He'd become part of the woods surrounding him, a strange and powerful force of nature contained in one perfect body. Power poured out from him, flowing over her, making her eyes water as the sun rose higher.

He pulled on his pants, stopped, and turned, spying her leaning against a tree, watching him. He turned that devastating smile to her and extended his hand. "What are you doing out here so early?" She could see his breath in the morning light, but he stood there in bare feet and no shirt.

She ran to him, taking his hand. "I was looking for you." Her voice trembled as she stared at him, still seeing him as he was before denim and cotton interfered. What was wrong with her? Why couldn't her voice ever come out strong any more?

"Really?" His amusement broke her out of the spell she'd stuck herself in. "Why?"

She sighed as he pulled her into his arms. His skin was warm, as warm as the dawn's light made him look. "I wanted to know if you had a chance to talk to our friend. He said he'd tell you what we talked about."

He held her close, stroking her hair. "Yeah. He told me everything." He raised an eyebrow. "Pins and needles, eh?"

She covered her face with her hands. "That's it! He's dead and then I'm joining him."

"It's all right, Karen." Randall pulled her hands down, his eyes sparkling with amusement. "Didn't he tell you my feelings are just like yours?"

"Well, yes, but it's not the same," she insisted. Her heart pounded as she watched his eyes light up. "I mean, you're the hero of this fairy tale. You're not supposed to have pins and needles. Only the poor heroine is allowed those kind of feelings."

He smoothed a stray strand of her hair back. "It *is*

the same. Pins and needles is the most accurate description I've heard for true love in years. And heroes, more often than not, feel the same things as the heroines. Don't let anyone tell you different." He pulled her tightly against his chest. "We'll have an end to our story, just like he told you."

His skin was smooth and hard, reminding her of a pebble worn down by water. "What if it's not the end we want?" Her arms snaked around his neck. "What happens if we can't save the children?"

"Don't worry about the future. Worry about now."

Randall felt so right in her embrace. He was more natural, more real to her than Bradford could ever hope to be. Her eyes closed when she felt him place a lingering kiss on her forehead. "That doesn't count, does it?"

He laughed. "No, there's only one that counts."

"I wish we could stay here forever," she whispered, gazing up at him.

"Soon." He brushed her hair away from her face. "As soon as I find the children. It won't be much longer."

A faint sound reached her. "Do you hear something? It sounds like music."

He stared at her. "You can hear it?" She nodded. "It's the wood folk. They're welcoming the new day. Humans can't usually hear it."

She laid her hands on the hard planes of his chest. "Maybe it's because I'm with you."

He led her to a large oak. Placing her hand against the trunk, he laid his over hers. "Can you hear it better?"

Karen cocked her head. "Yes. It's beautiful." She

swayed in time to the rhythms filling her. "It gets into you somehow." She noticed the trees looked fuller, the sunrise brighter, and all the noises surrounding her were amplified, clearer. "I've never seen the woods become so..."

"Alive," he finished. He pulled the heavy sweater from her and wrapped his arms around her, moving with her to the fairy music.

He drew her close, his chest pressing into her back, his arm resting under her breasts as he held her hand, guiding her feet through quick, intricate steps, their bodies moving as one. She closed her eyes, the feelings racing through her defying her every attempt to describe them. Sparks danced along her skin as his heat flowed into her, making her dizzy with desire. She tried to get nearer to him, to feel more of him against her.

She reached back, stroking his cheek with her fingertips. Laying her head back on his shoulder, she sighed when he caressed her neck with rough fingers. His hand moved upwards, smoothing her hair back. She gasped when his other hand made its way under her shirt to rest lightly on her stomach. His touch was light and heavy, cold and hot, rough and gentle. All without him moving one finger against her suddenly overly sensitive skin.

His bare chest warmed her back through her shirt as their dance continued. She could feel his hips press against her, quickening her breath. He laid his cheek on hers, the contact making her desire rise higher. He kissed her neck, sending fireworks shooting behind her eyelids. As he pulled her closer, she felt his need for her; it was tangible and alive, hanging in the air around them. She could feel it embrace her as his hands glided over her with a feather light touch.

Their steps made no sound as they moved across the leafy carpet. The fairy music built to a crescendo, sending her pulse racing, her temperature soaring, making her fear she would catch fire. He spun her away, then back, his hands drifting to her hips as he pulled her close.

The music faded as he ended the dance, bowing to her. He raised her hand to his lips. At his touch, Karen wondered how she was still standing. Her mouth was dry and her chest heaved as she struggled to suck air into her lungs, while parts of her body were screaming in protest at being ignored.

"I've never danced that way or felt like that before," she whispered.

"Welcome to my world." His voice had changed. It was deeper, fuller, more like her nighttime friend. He leaned closer.

This is it, she thought. Love's first kiss. She trembled as his mouth lowered to hers. She could feel the light fan of his breath against her face, could almost taste the sweetness of it. Her lips parted, her eyes fluttering closed. She could feel his lips just millimeters away.

"Randall!" a voice barked out.

They turned to see a very determined, very angry Raesheen striding toward them. "Did you forget you have things to see to?"

"No." He turned to Karen, running a finger along her jaw. "I suppose you'd better go. Raesheen's not in a good mood. I'll try to see you later."

Disappointment replaced the glow she'd had moments before. "All right." She caressed his face one more time. She turned to the dryad. "Good bye, Raesheen. It was nice seeing you again." She grabbed her sweater and jogged down the familiar path to the estate.

****

"At least she's properly respectful," Raesheen murmured. She stood in front of Randall, taking a hard swipe at his arm. "And you!" she shouted. "What in the name of Mother Earth were you thinking? You took her all the way through the Lovers Dance? Have you taken total leave of whatever sense you have left?"

Randall rubbed his arm where she hit him. Her slap stung, leaving small red scratches. "I couldn't help it. She heard the music and things just happened."

The dryad took a deep breath. "I know she's your soul mate. We all sensed it the moment she arrived," she said in a low voice. "But the Lovers Dance?" she shouted again. She glared at him, trying to make him see reason. "And then you were going to bestow love's first kiss? What's wrong with you? You can't use that kind of power at this point in time. When everything's over, I don't care what you do."

The corners of Randall's mouth twitched. "Are you done?" She was so much smaller than him and right now, so fierce, she reminded him of his young charges. "I guess I lost it there at the end."

She swatted him again, leaving more scratches. "Yes, you did. Rein in those rampant human hormones that fill you. We've got work to do." She paused, studying him in the light of the new day. "You haven't told her yet, have you?"

He glanced down the path to the mansion. "No."

What would Karen say when he finally showed her

that he was her night visitor? That all of her confessions about her feelings for him had been to him and not some third party?

"Smooth, Guardian," Raesheen said. "Very smooth. Let me know if she wants me to help her kick your butt."

Randall thought about his night conversations with Karen and all she'd said to him. "She's already threatened me with that."

This time, he didn't bother to hide the smile spreading across his face. He'd felt Karen's desire and was doing all he could to contain his. The strength and power of his soul mate's dragon spirit certainly confused his good judgment.

Chapter Nine

Karen crept into the drawing room, her sweater grasped in her hands. Randall's heat still filled her, making sweat bead on her forehead. She took a steadying breath, moving silently to the door. She opened it a crack and voices drifted to her. "Damn," she mouthed, hiding her presence from the group in the hall.

"I'm telling you, she suspects something," Edna said, her voice holding none of the kindness Karen had come to know. It was hard, edged with a cruelty she couldn't picture in the small, white-haired woman.

"It's true, sir," Cray said. "Wherever Dupré is, she's nearby. She's playing you."

"He's told her about the werewolves," Harmon added. "We've tried to lock up the guardian, but he always escapes and goes to her at night. The birds have seen them. He hasn't revealed his form to her yet. I think he's afraid she'll reject him when she sees the monster he is when the sun sets. It would be impossible to contain him when he's with her because that will raise all sorts of questions from her. I don't think she's one you want to tell about what's going on here."

"This is disturbing," Bradford said. "I wanted to keep her, but now it looks like we'll have to get rid of her with the others. Harmon, tell your animals to keep her under constant watch. Cray, do something about

Dupré. Edna, I expect positive results out of you, starting today. Bring the pack leader's son. He's the oldest, so his powers will be the most developed." He paused. "I want results. Get them."

Karen clamped a hand over her mouth as she listened to Bradford's retreating steps. She was more worried about the children than she was about herself. She'd had worse threats than this from people with a heck of a lot more power than him, so Bradford's words didn't scare her. She was going to have to be vigilant around him and his men and now Edna too.

She shook her head. They were all expendable. Time was growing short. Randall was close to saving the children, but close wasn't good enough. Not after what she'd just heard. Her mind began turning over possible plans to save them.

Her knuckles turned white as her fingers dug into the soft wool of her sweater. Karen slipped out the french doors and ran for the garden. She pulled her sweater over her head as her feet carried her to the bench by the fountain. Cold, sickening dread replaced Randall's warmth in her heart as Bradford's words haunted her. What did he mean when he told Edna to "get results"?

"If it were just me, it wouldn't be so bad," she murmured. "But Randall and the kids." She turned her face to the newly risen sun. "How do I help them?"

"You're not alone," said a tiny voice. "You have the fairies to help you."

Karen jumped to her feet. On the bench stood a tiny woman with yellow hair, her bare feet peeking out from beneath deep blue jeans, her translucent wings poking out through a Rush concert T-shirt. A golden glow surrounded her as she sat there.

Karen slowly sat back down. "Sorry. You startled me. Who are you?"

"I'm Dayla. Raesheen asked me to keep an eye on you." She stuck her hand out and Karen shook it, using her pinky finger. "I'm one of the wood folk."

"Karen."

"We know who you are." Dayla grinned. "You're the true love to one of us. Even though you're just a human, we're now duty-bound to protect you."

Karen shook her head. "Thanks." She looked at the cloudless sky. "I just wish things were simple again," she murmured.

The fairy cocked her head. "What was simple before true love?"

Karen watched the water in the fountain gurgle and run down its predestined path. "My friends and I working with law enforcement agencies to bring down some seriously bad people. Then we'd go home, regroup, and do it again. I like that life. I feel like I make a difference. But then my friend got married and everything changed."

Dayla's eyes grew as wide as a child's with a bedtime story. "Did she marry her true love?"

"I guess so." Karen glanced at her companion. "It certainly looked like true love to me."

The fairy stared at Karen, her eyes narrowing. "You aren't truly happy for her."

Karen felt tears build. "I am, really. I just didn't think I'd ever have a love like hers. I finally get that chance, and I can't even talk to him without looking over my shoulder, let alone do anything else."

"But he feels the same. All the realm knows it."

Dayla pirouetted. "And he did the Lovers Dance with you. That was so special."

Karen remembered the feel of him and the power that flowed from him as they danced in the early light. "I wished he'd kissed me when we finished. It felt right."

Dayla placed her tiny hand on Karen's. "Raesheen had good reason for stopping him. You can't unleash that much power with someone like Troyington nearby." She flew up to sit on Karen's shoulder. "He can sense strong magic."

"Great. He has his own powers," Karen mumbled. She turned to Dayla. "I know so little about your world. I didn't even think true love was real."

"Our world is not so different from yours." Dayla took to the air. "I will always be nearby if you need me. Troyington comes. Be careful."

She nodded and watched Dayla disappear. Forcing a smile to her face, she waved to Bradford. "Good morning," she called.

"We were worried when we couldn't find you." He took her hand, pulling her to her feet. He studied her intently, the look on his face saying he knew something was different about her.

"I was up before the sun and decided to watch the sunrise from the garden." She put her arm around his waist, trying to distract him. "I didn't mean to scare you."

He smiled at her, but it wasn't the same as the ones he'd given her before. She could feel him pulling away. He was even more distant than the previous evening. *If I don't do something, I'll lose him.*

She laid her head on his shoulder. "I really am

sorry, Bradford." She smiled at him, trying to win him back to her side. "Next time I'll leave a note."

He put his arm around her shoulders, not holding her as tightly. "It's time for breakfast, which is what started this whole looking-for-you situation."

As they entered the dining room, Edna ran to Karen, giving her a little shake. "You scared the life out of me. Where were you?"

"Outside, watching the sunrise. I'm sorry, Edna." Karen flinched slightly at the woman's touch. Having heard her earlier, she wondered what Edna had planned for her, for Randall, and most importantly, the children.

She shook her finger at Karen. "Don't do it again. I don't have much life to spare. So what are the two of you doing today?"

"If Karen will forgive me an hour or two, I have some important papers to fill out, but then I plan to spend all day with her," Bradford said.

Karen nodded. "Then I guess I'll just wander around until I have the pleasure of your company. What are you doing today, Edna?"

She smiled, an odd gleam sparkling in her eyes. "Oh, I have some things that will keep me out of mischief."

****

Karen waited until Bradford disappeared behind his study door and Edna left on her own business before heading outside. She meandered along, trying to appear like she was touring the grounds, but she was actually looking for Randall. She eyed the sky, not trusting the birds that flew over her head. She strolled down the hill to the stable and saw Cray go in, followed by Edna.

"So much for Edna staying out of mischief," she

mumbled. "What now?"

Drawing closer, she heard faint voices drifting from the end of the building. Crouching as she ran, she saw a small window open about halfway. She eased herself up to peer inside. A huge machine filled the room, crowding the desk and file cabinets to the side. It looked like it should be in a hospital, not an office in a stable.

Karen held herself perfectly still, calling on her power to cloud her presence from Troyington's people. She steadied her breathing, slowly turning her head to see what was happening.

Randall and a boy who looked to be in his late teens were strapped into chairs next to each other. The boy tried to put on a brave face, but Karen could almost smell his fear. From the look in Randall's eyes, she knew the trio was going to regret anything and everything they did now.

"What's going on?" the teen demanded.

"It's all right, James," Randall told him in a calm voice, his eyes never leaving Edna's face. "Just do what they say. They're not going to hurt you."

"That's right, dear," Edna said, patting him on the head. "We just need another few blood samples and to run a few more tests. Then you'll be taken back to the others."

"What're you going to do to the guardian?" James nodded at Randall.

Edna gestured at the tray of different sized scalpels. "You'll see. Won't it be fun to learn something new?"

Karen shivered as bile rose, burning the back of her throat. This wasn't the Edna she'd befriended. This woman was cruel, cold, and enjoyed terrorizing a young boy. Karen's instincts told her to get her butt in there and save them. Her head told her she'd better wait. Other opportunities would come to free James and the rest.

James had called Randall "guardian." Her nighttime friend had said he and Randall were brothers. In the light of the sunrise, Randall had certainly seemed more than human. After their dance, his voice had sounded like her night friend. If they were brothers, Randall must also hold the title of guardian. That would explain the power she felt in him.

She frowned. What if that wasn't entirely true? Could Randall *be* the guardian who came to her at night? She tried to deny it, but now that the thought was there, it wouldn't go away.

Edna placed several vials on the tray. "Now, James, I know your people can shift with or without the full moon." She smiled at him. "Evolution is a wonderful thing. I need a blood sample now, one in mid-shift, and one when you've fully changed."

James glared at her. "What if I don't? You can't make me."

"No, I can't," Edna said, preparing a syringe to draw blood. "But when you get back to the others, some of them might not be alive."

Randall turned to him. "It's okay. The others are depending on us."

James nodded and started shifting after Edna took the first vial of blood. His shoulders widened and his chest broadened, straining the straps of the chair restraints. The hair on his arms grew as his body turned more into its animal side. Faint cracks of bone sounded loud in the small room as James' body stretched, growing larger as he held both traits of human and wolf as Edna filled the second vial.

When she stood back, James pulled out more of the wolf. His hair lengthened as his legs began to resemble a wolf's, his feet and hands slowly changing themselves into large paws. He twisted to try and free himself, but a large hand clamped itself on the back of his neck and he growled, anger and hate coming from deep inside.

His face elongated into a blunt muzzle and eyes that held a hint of humanity glared out from the gray furred face. He tried to snap at who held him, but couldn't turn his head that far. His lips pulled back over white, pointed teeth as Edna filled her last vial.

James closed his eyes and reverted back to his human form. He rubbed his arm and watched as a bruise formed.

Randall nodded at him. "You did the right thing. Your father would be proud that you put pack safety ahead of your own."

"Thanks, Guardian."

"Now, Mr. Dupré, it's your turn." Edna pulled the machine into place as she put the scalpel tray in easy reach.

"What're you doing?" James demanded.

Edna slapped James, eliciting chuckles from Cray and Harmon. "I don't answer to you, boy. Now be quiet before I decide I don't need you any more."

"I won't let you hurt him." James started shifting again, and Cray clouted him hard on the side of the head. James turned human and he shook his head, trying to clear it. Cray hit him again, snapping his head back.

"Let me go to him," Randall said quietly to Edna.

"I promise, no tricks."

She opened the straps. "If you hadn't given me your word, you'd be out of luck."

He lifted the boy's face to inspect the damage and smiled at him. "Nothing serious, but you're going to have a real shiner later. I'm in no danger. They still need me." Randall turned, facing their enemies. "Take him back. He doesn't need to see this."

Cray grabbed a scalpel from the tray and held it to James' throat. "Beg for it."

Randall took a step forward, stopping when Cray pushed the scalpel harder into James' skin, his hands balling into fists. "I beg you to please take him back to the others."

Cray laughed. "No wonder the boss keeps you around." He shoved Randall back to the chair. "Sit, freak. It's going to be fun to watch you squirm."

"Take the boy back, Harmon," Edna ordered. "He's just a distraction now." She stood in front of Randall. "Your charges are undisciplined."

Randall glared at her. "It's hard for me to teach them anything when I'm not allowed to see them."

"Keep up with that attitude and you'll never see them again." Edna picked up a scalpel. "Now, let's try this again. Today I'm testing your regeneration. I'll need to take more samples from you later."

Randall's lip curled back in a snarl, and he pulled at the straps holding him in the chair. "You've taken samples of everything I've got in me. What else could you possibly want?"

Edna's gaze dropped to his lap. "Not everything. I haven't even started getting in to how you people reproduce."

Karen clamped a hand over her mouth, hoping to stem the full blown nausea that consumed her. Breakfast was in real danger of making a return appearance. She took several deep breaths. "Dayla, are you here?" she called in a hoarse whisper.

The fairy appeared, snapping off a salute. "Always, miss. How can I help?"

"There's a man coming out of this building with a teenage boy. Follow them. The boy is the pack leader's son. Find out where they're going and tell Raesheen." Karen stared at the window. Voices drifted to her, telling her she had to look. "I have to stay here in case Randall needs me."

"I'm on it." Dayla turned invisible, taking off after Harmon and James.

Karen peered in the window to see Edna turning some of the knobs that stuck out from the side. The large lens bending over the table moved back and forth, up and down while she tried to get the focus right.

"Cray, when I start, you'll need to hold his arm straight out under the lens. Get the clipboard please. We'll need to document everything."

"Sure, Dr. Strathmore." Cray handed her the clipboard with her notes and glared at Randall, his lips curling in a cruel smile. "This is going to hurt, southern boy. And I'm going to love every minute of it."

Karen watched Randall's eyes narrow as his mouth pulled down in a fierce scowl. Cray had better watch himself. When the werewolf children were safe, paybacks were definitely coming.

Edna picked up a small scalpel. "Let's see what we can see. We'll start with a shallow cut and go from there." She leveled a stern gaze at Randall. "I'd like for this session to go smoother than last one."

Cray walked behind Randall, smacking the back of his head before freeing one of his arms. "You heard the lady. Screw this up again and I'll twist the head off one of those kids."

Randall's eyes grew as hard and cold as the ice they resembled. Cray took a step back as Randall's stare bored holes through him. "If one child is harmed, there won't be enough left of you for people to mourn over. Do you understand me?"

Cray turned pale and fear clouded his eyes. He started to nod when Edna shoved him toward the end of the machine.

"Enough of this," she snapped. "Let's begin."

Edna drew the scalpel down Randall's arm in a shallow cut. "Surface skin heals almost instantaneously. I'm making a cut about a half an inch deeper."

Edna pushed the blade deeper into his arm. Randall's cheek twitched at the pain, but he made no sound. Cray stood across from him, smiling at his discomfort as he held his arm in a tight grip.

Edna stared into the scope as she made a two inch slice. "Amazing. The cut is still fresh, but the blood flow has already slowed. This is absolutely remarkable." She turned to the instrument tray behind her and selected a scalpel with a longer blade. "Let's try a little deeper. Cray, hold him securely for this one. And turn his arm over. I need a fresh area."

Karen watched as Cray turned Randall's arm so his palm was facing up. Blood still seeped from the cut on the other side, pooling under his elbow. Movement from the house caught her eye. Bradford marched toward the stable, his cell phone pressed to his ear and he was shouting at the person on the other end.

He flung open the office door, heading straight for Randall, backhanding him. "Your northeast clan just destroyed one of my research labs," he shouted.

Blood trickled from the corner of Randall's mouth. "So why take it out on me?" he growled, his voice shaking with pain and rage. "Go find the clan and tell them how displeased you are with them retaliating when you harm those close to them."

Bradford hit him again. "Because you're all I've got." He turned to Edna. "Are you making any progress with him?"

"I'm mapping the process his skin undergoes during regeneration." Edna handed him the clipboard. "This is just from today. I have to compile all my data, but things look very good. I should have the shape-shifter serum in another couple of weeks, the regeneration formula before that. I may have to dissect some of the children in different stages of the change so I can see how the internals work." She nodded in Randall's direction. "We should be done with him in another week."

Bradford nodded. "I agree. Use the older brats." He glared at Randall. "Getting rid of you will be a pleasure."

"And to think I believed we had nothing in common," Randall growled.

Edna jotted some notes on the clipboard. "I need to make one last deep cut on him to record how the muscle tissue knits together and then I'm done."

"Troyington, listen to me," Randall said, needing to say something, anything to stop them from hurting his charges. "If you kill any of the children, the pack won't care any more. They'll descend on you. They'll rip you apart." Randall bared his teeth at his captor as his voice dropped to a deep rumble. "And if they don't, I will."

Bradford turned back to Edna. He picked up the longest blade she had, studying it in the bright sunlight filtering in through the window. "You need to make one more cut? Let me help."

He drove the scalpel straight down through Randall's arm so it scratched the table underneath, smiling as Randall cried out. "Don't threaten me, Guardian. I'm seriously considering letting none of you live."

Blood splashed over the table, as Randall's fingers twitched and veins stood out on his neck. Troyington pushed the scalpel in deeper, then yanked it out. Randall's arm jerked as he tried to pull it out of Cray's grip.

"Not yet, boy. The doctor's still studying you," the handyman said, squeezing his arm harder, making him cry out again.

Karen closed her eyes as she turned away, unable to stand watching them torture him any longer.

"I'm done," she heard Edna say. "Get him out of here before his blood ruins my equipment."

Randall hit the ground at the stable entrance and Karen ran to him. Casting a nervous glance over her shoulder, she yanked him to his feet and pulled him into the woods.

She eased him down next to a small, gurgling stream. Sunlight streamed through the trees, shining on the water. A bird's call sounded, and she spared it a quick look before focusing on Randall. "How could they do that to you?"

"It's what they do," he said, cradling his bleeding arm. The pain in his voice made his drawl sound thicker than usual. Blood smeared his pants. "Damn it, this is my best pair of jeans."

"Can I do anything?" She made herself sit there instead of running back to hurt them as badly as they'd hurt him. She wiped her eyes, cursing the tears that blurred her vision. She could feel her emotions breaking out of the internal bottle she'd stuffed them into.

"I've got it covered." He dipped his fingers into the clear water. "Brek, I could use your help." He angled his head to look at Karen. "Are you crying?"

She ignored him, choosing to inspect his arm instead. "That blade went all the way through, but the blood's almost stopped." The first cut Edna had made was already fading. "Regeneration, huh?"

He sat back, staring at the stream as the water began to swirl and bubble. "Yeah. It's how my race has lived so long." He turned her head to him, brushing a tear away with his thumb. "Don't cry. It's not as bad as it seems." He gave a snort of laughter. "They've done worse to me."

Karen just nodded. She'd wanted to save him, save them both, but she'd just watched. A cold hand clamped around her heart. Feeling powerless was new to her and she didn't like it.

Randall started to speak when a beautiful woman rose out of the stream. "How can I be of service to you, my friend?" Her body, her hair, even her dress were all made from the stream she floated in.

He held his arm out for her to see. "They stuck a

scalpel in me, Brek. Strathmore was studying my regeneration, then she had me thrown in the dirt. Can you clean it out?" He brushed away some of the dust, crying out when he hit the cut.

She gently held his arm. "Of course. Hold still." She held her hands above and below the wounds, water pouring from her fingers as she washed out the cuts.

He sucked air through his teeth. "Damn, that hurts."

She laughed, the sound reminding Karen of fast running rivers or a small waterfall. "You've had a knife stuck through your arm. It's supposed to hurt. The cold water will help with the pain. If it's possible, keep it clean. I know how you are. Sometimes I think you are more child than man."

Randall grinned. "You just say that because you're hundreds of years older than me." He flexed his arm, making blood ooze out.

"Yes, I am, and I would wish for a little more respect from you." She turned her attention to Karen. "She's the one we felt?"

Randall nodded, taking Karen's hand. "Karen, this is Brek. She's a water nixie. Brek, this is Karen."

The nixie stretched herself out to surround Karen, looking at her from all angles. She flowed back to the steam, satisfied by what she found. "She's a lovely person, inside and out. I approve."

He watched Karen walk away, her shaking shoulders telling him she was crying. "What's wrong?"

Karen kept her back to them. "How can the two of you treat this so lightly?" She glanced over her shoulder. "Randall, they tortured you. You've been stabbed and I just stood there. I'm as bad as they are."

She turned and stared at them.

She wiped at her face with her hands. "Every time I've fought someone or helped with a rescue operation, I've always known what to do. This time, nothing. I stood there and watched and did nothing."

He pulled her into his arms, raising her face to his. "Listen to me. Anything you could've done or tried to do, would've gotten you caught or killed and made things worse for me."

She stared at the ground. "When Harmon came out with the boy, I wanted to follow him, but I couldn't leave you. I sent Dayla after them instead."

"Karen, look at me." He gazed tenderly at her, smiling when she finally raised her eyes to his. "That was the best thing you could've done. Dayla is Raesheen's chief tracker." He wiped her tears away, gently caressing her face. "See? You knew exactly what to do."

"Oh?" Karen's voice trembled.

His power rose around them, pouring into her. "Yes. If you'd gone after Harmon, then this wouldn't have happened."

She trembled as he lowered his mouth to hers.

Chapter Ten

Electricity shot through her entire body, tingling her nerves and sending her soul soaring. Blood raced through her veins as his power poured into her and moved around her, caressing her. And her blood wasn't just singing, it was belting out the "Hallelujah Chorus." She felt his heart thump against her breasts as hers began to pound in time to his rhythm. She could smell the wild magic that filled him even as she tasted it on her lips.

She twined her arms around his neck, reveling in the hardness of his chest and arms as he held her. Her skin flamed everywhere he touched her. She sighed into his mouth as he pulled her closer, deepening the kiss they finally shared.

"Randall, *no*!" Raesheen dashed into the clearing, grabbing Randall by his hair and yanking his head back.

"*Ow*! Raesheen, cut it out!" He pried the dryad off his scalp, setting her on the ground.

"How could you?" she screamed. "You promised me you'd wait. Do you realize what you've done?"

Randall's eyes hardened as he glared at his friend. "Yes, I do. You approved of her. I've got the High Mother's blessing and the Oracle said it was to be. What's the problem?"

"*The problem*?" she shouted. "You have the nerve to ask me that?"

Karen moved in between the two of them, wondering if they were going to come to blows. "I don't understand. What's going on?"

"I'll tell you the problem and everything else." Raesheen stalked toward her, stabbing her finger at Randall. "This idiot has just bound himself to you. He's not only shared love's first kiss, but he shared his power. He promised me he'd wait until this situation was settled."

She frowned. "I still don't get it."

"Be calm," Brek said, her gaze darting back and forth between them. "She's still learning our ways."

Raesheen squeezed her eyes shut and stomped her foot. "I am calm!"

She pulled Karen out of Randall's embrace, yanking her arm hard enough to make her sit on the hard ground. "If he's dumb enough to get himself killed before you two consummate your relationship, the power he just gave you will rip you apart. You won't have a chance to die of a broken heart because his power will consume you until there's nothing left."

The dryad stalked back over to him, kicking him squarely in the shins. "That's why he promised me he'd wait!"

Randall leaned down, rubbing his leg. "Do you have to wear combat boots?"

"Yes. They serve an extremely practical purpose for kicking you." She folded her arms and turned her back to him. "And I like the sound they make when they connect with your anatomy."

Randall sat next to Karen and pulled her into his arms. "I'm sorry. I should've waited like Raesheen said. I've put you in danger."

She shrugged, smiling slightly. "No more than I usually am. Of course, the thought of death by power consumption isn't doing anything for me." She ran her hands down his chest to the waistband of his jeans. "We can fix that, you know."

"I know." He leaned closer to her, intent on another soul searing kiss.

"Enough." Raesheen pushed them apart. "Please have some consideration for the rest of us. Karen, you must get back to the house. Troyington will be looking for you soon. Aren't you two supposed to spend the day together?"

"Yes, we are." She caressed Randall's face, not wanting to leave his embrace. "You won't be dumb enough to get yourself killed, will you?"

"Of course not. I promise." He grinned. Her cheeks turned pink as she gazed into his eyes. "Remind me to smile at you more."

"*Focus!*" the dryad screamed.

"I'm sorry." Karen looked at Randall. "I think I'm distracting you. I'd better get back. Bradford might be looking for me by now."

"You must be careful," the dryad said. She grasped Karen's arm. "You must act the same as you did before that fool over there ruined everything."

Karen winked at Raesheen. "But he's a cute fool."

The dryad snorted. "Why do you think I've let him live this long?"

Karen chuckled before covering Raesheen's hand with her own. "I'll remember all you told me. My friend has already told me the consequences of what Troyington will do us if he finds out Randall and I are soul mates."

Night Angel

"Remember, Troyington senses magic. Hold Randall's power tight inside you and if you're lucky, Troyington won't detect it. Keep your wits, and he'll never suspect you've lost your heart." She glanced over her shoulder at Randall. "We have work to do. Good luck."

"Same to you." With a last look at the group behind her, Karen headed for the mansion, hoping she could pull off the biggest charade of her life.

****

"I've been looking for you," Bradford said as he entered the library. "I'm finally caught up on everything I need to be."

Karen rose out of the leather wingback chair, holding up a book. "I wandered around outside for a bit then came in here. I borrowed this book. Do you mind?"

He took her hands and kissed her cheek. "Of course not. What would you like to do today?"

After what she'd overheard that morning, she felt he was studying her, paying closer attention than usual to what she'd say. "Let's go to that little town down the hill from here."

He smiled. "That's a great idea. I haven't taken an afternoon off in ages. Get your things and I'll pull the car around front."

"I'll be down in just a minute."

Karen ran to her room. "Dayla, are you here?"

"Always," said the fairy, appearing on her pillow.

Karen stuffed things into her purse. "Did you find out where Harmon took the boy?"

"He put him in the back of a closed truck." Dayla hung her head. "He drove so fast, I lost him. I alerted the rest of the Court to try to pick up his trail. I tracked him as far as I could and he led me away from the hills, not toward them."

Karen chewed her lip. "That must mean the cabin they plan on using isn't ready yet. I don't think we're going to be able to rescue the kids until they're in place. Edna is close to completing her serum for Bradford." She grabbed her jacket from the closet doorknob. "We've got a week, maybe two, to wrap this up."

Dayla stood ramrod straight and saluted. "I will report all of this to Raesheen at once."

"When you get to the wood folk, tell them I'm getting Bradford out of the house for a few hours. They might be able to get into his private office while we're gone." Karen stuffed her arms in her jacket sleeves, glancing toward the door. "I've got to run. Be careful."

"You too, miss."

She grabbed her purse and made her way to the car waiting for her outside.

****

The stores in the town were all on the single main road running through the center. Karen thought this was the cleanest town she'd ever been in. The sidewalks looked swept, no grass in the cracks; the road had no potholes or big dips or bumps. She watched as people bustled in and out of the shops and drove by them, hurrying off to where they needed to be. It appeared to be a normal, small town. *So why does it feel like I've just stepped into the Twilight Zone?*

Bradford kept Karen's hand in his as they strolled through the little town's shopping district. He called out greetings, waving to everyone they met. He pointed out various important buildings, sounding proud of the

Night Angel

town hall.

Karen watched him wave to another couple passing them on the street. "Do you know everyone?"

"I helped the people here when I first moved in," he said. "The town was on the verge of drying up. I moved in some companies, built a few new businesses, created some jobs, and now it's a prosperous place to live."

She watched the people walk by. "That was awfully nice of you to help out complete strangers."

He shrugged. "It was pure selfishness on my part. The next town is over twenty miles away. I didn't want to have to go that far."

"I don't blame you. It'd be murder in the winter." Karen looked at the streets. "The roads are so narrow."

Bradford turned to speak with a woman who approached them. She looked at Karen like she wasn't good enough to breathe the same air as the man with her. As Karen gazed at the other locals, she got the same sort of reaction. She could feel the hair on the back of her neck rise.

The wood folk hadn't made her feel like this when she met them. They'd welcomed her as one of their own even though the only tie she had with them was through Randall. She shoved the thought down, making herself think of anything but Randall. If she kept thinking like that, she'd tip her hand. She smiled at him when he glanced at her.

She waited until the woman moved off. "They certainly think a lot of you here. I think they resent me being with you."

Bradford tightened his grip on her hand. "They never think anyone is good enough for me. They put me on a pedestal even though I tell them I'm just a regular citizen like them."

She resisted the urge to pull her hand from his. "I think they see you as a little more than that, if you don't mind me saying." She let him put his arm around her. His arm made her feel like a prisoner, but from the looks she was getting, right now, she'd take any kind of protection. The feelings of the townspeople bothered her. If they ever found the children, she got the feeling there would be no help here.

He stared at her, the look in his eyes sending a chill up her spine. His hand tightened on her shoulder. "They'd do anything I'd ask of them. They don't put up with people trying to get the better of me."

Karen's feet wanted to run away and take her with them, but didn't want to let him see how his veiled threat shook her. She gave him a bright smile. "Nice to have that kind of loyalty, huh? I'm starving! Could we stop for a quick bite?"

"This cafe is nice and quiet. The food here is delicious." He gently pushed her into the dim interior, guiding her to a back table. "I hope you're having a good time."

"Oh, yes. It's a lovely town and the people like you so much." She held his hand. "You're a special man, Bradford. I'm glad I've had time to get to know you."

If they handed out Academy Awards for lying through your teeth, I'd get one, hands down.

****

Karen stared at the tree. She didn't hear any rustling of leaves or creaking of branches. Maybe he was late. She watched as several blackbirds landed on the overhanging branches as they watched her. She moved down the balcony away from them.

Raesheen leapt from a tree branch onto the balcony. She turned to the birds and stared at them for a moment before dismissing them with a wave of her hand. "He's not coming."

"Is he all right?" Karen sat on the balcony, leaning against the house as her mind conjured up all sorts of horrible things that could've happened to him or Randall. "Has something happened?"

The dryad chuckled. "Both are well. They send their regards and their apologies. They slipped away from Troyington's men and wanted to see if there was anywhere else the children could be hidden on the estate. After what Dayla told us this afternoon, I believe you're right. As soon as I have word the children are where we expect them to be, I'll let you know."

Karen shuddered, remembering her afternoon out. "I'm afraid we're all running out of time. I think Bradford is suspicious I'm not falling in love with him. He made a lot of veiled threats today, directing most of them at me." She got up, walking to the rail to peer into the darkness beyond. "Maybe the guardian was right. I should've never come back."

"Why did you?" Raesheen tilted her head, staring at Karen. "Most humans would've fled at the first opportunity, yet you returned."

"I'm in love with Randall. I loved him even before we kissed," she whispered. Karen closed her eyes, turning her back to the fairy queen. "The first night he looked in my car, I felt a connection with him. He was strange and wild and perfect. Then, after seeing what he's endured, all for the sake and safety of others, how could I not return? I love him, Raesheen. I need him."

The dryad nodded. "I understand."

Karen leaned on the rail, laying her head back and opened her eyes to stare at the stars. "Ever since we started bonding, everything looks better. Bigger. Brighter. How are things going to look once we're permanently together? And are we even going to get to be together?"

Raesheen stroked Karen's hair, trying to give her some kind of comfort. "Love's first kiss isn't supposed to cause more problems. It's supposed to make things better," she said, her voice soft as an evening breeze. "It's a terrible situation we're in. But the High Mother has promised we'll succeed."

"Who's the High Mother?" Karen asked, too tired to even try not sounding tired.

Raesheen sat on the railing by Karen's arm. "She's the leader of Randall's clan. Her Oracle had visions of the future."

"Oh?" Karen stared at the dryad. "Did I have something to do with his future?"

"The Oracle saw Randall meeting a silver dragon. He confessed to me he saw the dragon spirit in you. The High Mother dreamed of you." Raesheen held Karen's arm in a tight grip. "You're the reason Randall was chosen to be here. He was meant to find you. You two are meant to be together."

"It'd be nice if we could actually *be* together," Karen muttered. She turned to Raesheen. "Do you believe we'll succeed? Do you think we'll get happily ever after?"

"The High Mother said so. She hasn't been wrong yet." Raesheen smiled. "And the Oracle wouldn't let her brother come to harm."

Randall had a sister that could see the future. *Not surprising*, she thought. Surely, the Oracle would've known if he wouldn't succeed and wouldn't have let him come. Wouldn't she? *This gets more confusing all the time*, she thought.

"I'm afraid," Karen said in a low voice. Tears spilled, splashing on the wooden railing. "I'm afraid of him. I'm afraid *for* him. I'm really afraid of this all-consuming love that has me walking on eggshells." She slammed her hands on the rail, making the dryad jump. "Damn it!"

"I know it's hard." Raesheen squeezed her shoulder. "Something deep and primal is beginning to control your life. In this type of situation, soul bonding can hurt."

Karen stared at the ground. "I feel so fractured."

The dryad stood back, folding her arms and Karen could feel her annoyance. "That's Randall's fault. You're supposed to be able to consummate after sharing love's first kiss. *Then* he's supposed to share his power." She tried to frown, but the corners of her mouth turned up in a smile. "He never could do anything right without me to guide him. That's why he promised me he'd wait."

Her eyes narrowed as she gazed intently at Karen. "I know why he didn't, though. He couldn't. I've never sensed a love this strong before. It resonates through the entire realm."

Karen wiped her eyes. It figured when she finally let her emotions out, it would be like that. The constant crying was driving her nuts. "What do we do? I can't go on like this."

The dryad shook her head. "There's not much we

can do. If you two do consummate the bond, Troyington will definitely know, and he'll get rid of you." She hopped off the railing to pace on the balcony. "He won't get rid of Randall, not right away, because he still needs to take his power. But you. Troyington will see you as expendable. I'm not sure what he'll do, but it won't be pretty."

"Terrific." Karen sat on the porch. "This true love thing stinks. And I thought it was hard being a hero."

Raesheen patted her arm. "It'll get better."

The look Karen gave her was beyond skeptical. "Oh, yeah? How?"

"It's a fairy tale, not an opera."

Karen wished she could believe the dryad, but she'd read too many stories where things didn't go as planned. Would that happen to her? She hoped not, but things had a way of getting too far out of control too quickly.

"Please give us a happily ever after," she silently prayed.

Chapter Eleven

"You seem different this morning," Bradford said, piling scrambled eggs on his plate.

"Do I?" Karen stamped on the now familiar panic rising in her chest. She wished she could regain her focus, but had a feeling it was long gone. The closer she got to Randall, the more out of control her emotions became. "How?" She took several small bites of her breakfast, feeling them sit heavy in her stomach.

"I'm not sure, exactly, but I mean to find out." He leaned over to her. "I hope it's nothing serious."

Karen wiped her mouth to stop her hands from shaking. "Maybe it's because I met a wonderful man who thinks the world of me."

He turned a cold smile to her and she felt it slice through her. "I hope you mean *me*."

"Who else could I mean?" She laid her hand over his. "I haven't spent time with anyone else."

He filled her coffee cup and grabbed another piece of toast for himself. "That's good to hear. My employees are under a different impression."

Karen's knees shook under the table. "Oh?"

He nodded. "They seem to think you have feelings for Dupré." He stared at her. "Do you?"

She gestured to the dining room, sweeping her arms wide to indicate the whole house. "Why would I want anyone else when you have all this?"

He sat back, apparently satisfied and pointed to her plate. "Are you done?"

She glanced at the remainder of her breakfast and put her napkin on the table. "Yes, I am."

"Good." He stood, pulling her chair out for her. "I have a surprise for you today."

"I love surprises." Karen frowned when he walked away from her, not taking her arm, her hand, or touching her in any way. *This can't be good*, she thought.

He led her to the study. He pulled out a long black box from the top drawer of his desk and held it out to her.

Karen opened it and gasped at the sight of a large ruby pendant attached to a thin gold chain lying on a bed of satin, shimmering in the morning sun filtering through the windows. "Oh, Bradford, it's beautiful."

He removed the necklace, hooking it around Karen's neck. "By accepting this, you promise I have your complete loyalty."

"I don't understand," she said, frowning. Not good, she told herself again. "What do you mean?"

"Come with me." He opened the french doors, stepping out into the morning air and slowly gazed around the estate. Wispy clouds drifted across the pale blue sky, the autumn sun weakly shining. The trees were mostly bare now, a sure sign winter was on its way. "It's getting colder. It'll be winter before we know it."

Karen took a deep breath. "Bradford, are you okay?" He'd been different since their trip to town. Heck, it had started before that when his employees told him about her and Randall.

"I'm fine. Let's see how you fare in the next few minutes." He grabbed her arm, marching her down to the stable. "Yesterday, I felt something powerful reverberate through me. I know what's happened between you and Dupré."

Karen yanked her arm from his hard grip. "What are you talking about?" He'd felt them bond with that first intense kiss? "Nothing's happened."

"I have no magical powers myself, but I can sense it when it's being used. My mother knew I could feel magic and taught me to attune myself to the energies of the earth." He grabbed her again, pulling her down the hill.

"Sounds interesting," she said.

"It is. Soul bonding is the most primal, most powerful magical force out there." He stopped and jerked her around to face him. "I know what the two of you have done."

Karen used every ounce of willpower she possessed to not shake as she saw anger fill his eyes. "We haven't done anything." She wanted to run from him, but her legs wouldn't cooperate.

His smile was cold, freezing her soul. "We'll see," he said. "We'll see."

Bradford pushed her through the stable doors. As her eyes adjusted from the glare of the sun, she felt as if the floor had collapsed under her feet. Her blood turned to ice at the sight of Randall hanging from a large hook, his arms stretched over his head, hands bound, his bare feet barely touching the floor. He'd been stripped to the waist, his arms and stomach covered with what looked like burns. Her stomach churned from the smell of wet hay and horse. She swallowed hard, trying to keep everything where it was supposed to be.

Karen's first impulse was to run to Randall, but the look in his eyes warned her to keep herself in check. She turned and glared at Bradford. "What are you doing? Cut him down, right now!"

Bradford gestured for Harmon to come over. The stable master showed her the metal bar in his hands. "My animals have told me those that live in the fairy world can't stand this." He hefted the bar in front of her face.

"What is it?" she asked, her eyes fixed on the metal rod.

"Cold iron." Harmon smiled and looked over his shoulder at Randall. "Magical creatures can't bear its touch. It can make them sick or even kill them. Depends on how long they're in contact with it. It poisons them, you see?"

Bradford placed both hands on Karen's shoulders, holding her in place. "Show her, Harmon."

Harmon walked over to Randall and quickly touched the bar to his outstretched arm. Randall howled and tried to jerk away. His skin blistered where Harmon had laid the rod. Harmon touched him again, laughing as Randall tried to twist away from him. His body broke out in a thin sheen of sweat as another area turned red, his flesh bubbling.

Karen pulled out of Bradford's grasp. "Just what are you trying to prove with this demonstration?"

"I want to see for myself you have no feelings for him." He shrugged, his eyes cold. "Tell me that's true and I'll cut him loose."

"I told you this morning, I have *you*. I don't need anyone else." She grabbed Bradford's jacket. "He has nothing. You've got everything. You even gave me this beautiful necklace. He's never given me anything."

Bradford pushed her over to stand in front of Randall. "Look at him. Say you have no feelings for him. Tell him to his face and if you two have formed any bonds, they'll begin to break. If you say nothing, I'll know you do care for him and steps will have to be taken."

She could see Randall's eyes begging her to say it. If she did, she'd save their lives, but break both their hearts. Her mind raced with alternatives. *How do we get out of this one?*

Harmon approached, raising the bar and slamming it into Randall's side, enjoying his screams as the metal contacted his skin. The sickly sweet smell of burned flesh filled the stable. Karen kicked her leg out sending the iron rod skittering across the barn floor. She threw her left arm up, blocking Harmon's swing at her head. Her right came up, catching the left side of Harmon's face, knocking him to the ground.

Harmon surged to his feet, charging her. Karen waited until the last moment, then stepped to the side and threw him to the ground again. He grabbed her ankle and she kicked him loose then turned to Bradford.

"Are all you people out of your minds?" she shouted. "You really believe fairies and magic are real? I don't know what that bar is treated with, but I'm sure it has to be some type of acid." She yanked on the knotted rope, untying it and letting Randall fall to the floor. "Torture is illegal in the States, Bradford." She pointed at Randall. "You're lucky he hasn't gone to the authorities with accounts of your abuse."

Randall climbed to his feet, and she shoved him

toward the door. "Get out, Dupré. If you would just do your job around here and quit spreading malicious rumors about me, none of this would've happened."

She stalked over to Bradford, taking off the necklace and stuffing it into his hand. "And you. How could you treat me like this? Keep your necklace! I'm going home!" Karen slammed the door open and stormed up the hill to the house. *How long until he realizes I never denied Randall?*

"That was wonderfully played, miss," Dayla said next to her right ear.

Karen's gaze searched for Randall. "Thanks," she muttered.

The fairy smiled as she watched Karen. "He sent me to you. He said he's fine and not to worry. He enjoyed watching you kick Harmon."

"But the burns." She chewed her lip as she thought about the pain he'd endured. "Will he heal?"

"Yes. He may not even scar." Dayla looked over her shoulder. "Troyington comes. Be strong, miss."

"Karen, wait!"

She stopped and turned, folding her arms, glaring at him as he approached. "Why? That was insulting and humiliating. I'm serious, Bradford. I'm leaving as soon as I can get packed."

"Just let me apologize for my actions. Here." He held the necklace out to her. "Take it. Please."

"I don't know why I should." She eyed the necklace, knowing Bradford wasn't going to let this matter drop so easily.

"I'm sorry. I shouldn't have put you through that or let my man hurt Dupré in that fashion." He gave her a small smile. "Please take it?"

She took the necklace from his hand, fastening it around her neck. "One more incident like this, and I promise you, no more chances. I'll be out of here before you've realized I've left."

He kissed her cheek. "It's a deal." He moved closer, his eyes narrowing. "And for your end of it, stay away from Dupré and all will be forgiven."

They started walking toward the house, Bradford's hand on her elbow. "I can't help run into him here," she told him. "We're on the same estate."

He glanced at her, his face hard and unreadable. "Don't worry. I've come up with a way around that particular problem."

Dread crawled up her spine. *What was he planning?* She wiped her hands on her pants as they headed up the small hill to the house and made a silent vow. *I swear, if we live through this, I'll never be jealous again.*

He was silent for a moment. "You really don't believe in magic?"

She sighed, weighing her response. "It was a childhood fantasy. It's nice to pretend, but in the end, reality has to take over."

If she came right out and said she didn't believe in magic, would she lose all her new friends as well as the man she loved? This was getting a little too tricky.

He watched her closely as he led her toward the house. "What would you like to do today?"

"I think I want some time to myself." She stopped at the porch. "I'm going to take a walk around the grounds for a bit. I'm still considering going home."

He narrowed his eyes. "Take all the time you need. I'll be in my regular study if you want to see me."

She watched him retreat to the house. As soon as he disappeared, she wandered toward the garden. She heard birds calling to each other and eyed them as they flew over her head. She noticed squirrels following her as she walked to the bench by the fountain.

"Dayla, are you here?" she called quietly.

The fairy appeared next to her on the bench. "I'm always nearby, miss. What can I do?"

Karen watched the birds circling overhead. "Is he still safe?"

Dayla nodded. "He wants to be with you so badly, miss, but doesn't dare show himself." She looked around. Animals scampered nearby, stopping to glance at them and she shivered.

"The animals are still watching me," Karen murmured. "Why hasn't Harmon's hold on them been broken yet? Is he really that much more powerful than you guys?"

Dayla shook her head. "His control is almost absolute. He has a knack for talking to animals that has nothing to do with his power. They trust him, and his power lets him into their minds." The fairy shrugged. "All we have is magic."

Karen ground her teeth, frustrated by not being able to help the people she counted as friends. "But fairies have been around for a long time. Shouldn't old magic be stronger than one paranormal human?"

"Not really." Dayla sat down near her. "This isn't the first time we've seen the animals of the world controlled by someone." Her hands balled into tiny fists. "We exist alongside the animals. We don't control them or tamper with them in any way. The animals don't realize they're being controlled, so it makes the compulsion hard to break."

Karen looked at her. "Why?"

"It's not mind control so much as Harmon giving their instincts a boost." Dayla flew up to sit on her shoulder. "He's just nudging them in the direction he wants them to go."

Another fairy flew up and whispered to Dayla. She turned and saw Randall standing at the edge of the woods and flew to him. "What can I do for you, guardian?"

"I need to speak with Karen." He eyed the birds overhead and the small creatures running through the garden. "Tell her to wander over here and see if you can distract the blackbirds. The others I'm not that concerned about, but the birds are smart and they're Harmon's main source of information."

Dayla grinned and took off. She reached Karen and nodded toward the woods where Randall was hiding. Karen walked through the garden, wandering closer to his spot. She watched Dayla punch a blackbird on the beak and then fly off at high speed.

Randall stayed under the tree canopy and Karen kept her gaze on the flowers bouncing in the breeze. "We don't have much time," he said in a low voice.

She glanced at him before stooping to smell some late blooming flowers. "You're vulnerable to cold iron?"

"Every race has their own Achilles heel. Those of us in the fairy realm have cold iron." As she moved down the outside row, he went with her, staying out of sight of the birds circling overhead. "Harmon was right, you know. It can kill us. It's how they killed the guardians that came here first to rescue the children."

She frowned. "How? I'm trying to understand, Randall, but every time I get an answer, I get twenty more questions."

He nodded. "I know. Troyington had a cold iron dagger specifically made for my race," he explained. "When our skin comes in contact with it, well, you saw what happens. If it gets in our blood, it poisons us. Leave the blade in and it can kill us it minutes." He paused. "Troyington stabbed two of the guardians he took captive and tortured the others. He was going to kill me, too, but Strathmore told him she could replicate my powers and abilities and transfer them to him. That's why they kept me alive. They keep trying to keep me locked up at night but aren't having much luck."

"I'm so sorry," she whispered.

"It's all right," Randall said. "Soon, this will all be concluded and Troyington will pay for his crimes against the northeast pack. If his brother was here, none of this would be going on."

Karen glanced at him, then turned back to the garden in front of her. "Why? Is he someone important?"

"From what I've found out, his brother was disowned by their parents, and he and Troyington can't stand the sight of each other. Unfortunately, he's out of the country right now with some kind of medical condition that needs serious treatment."

A blackbird's raucous call sounded shattered the stillness and Randall lifted his head to watch it come closer. "I have to go. They'll tell Harmon they saw me if they get any closer."

Her chest tightened at his words. *I'm getting tired*

of always being afraid. It wasn't fear for herself, but the fear of what would happen to the man who held her heart that made this now familiar panic constantly claw at her guts.

She looked up at the blackbird flying overhead. "Are you in danger?"

"No more than usual. It's you I'm worried about."

She glanced over her shoulder and smiled. "I can take care of myself. What I did to Harmon is only a tiny sample of what I can do."

"We've got to stay away from each other. Every second we're together puts you in danger."

She gave in to the trembling that constantly threatened her. "I'm afraid for you. Bradford told Cray to deal with you. He told Edna to get results."

"I can handle those two. Cray might be strong, but he's got a soft spine. Edna may think she's untouchable, but she isn't. As for Harmon, well, the wood folk's magic is beginning to crack his hold. The more they push, the more concentration he needs to exert to control the animals in the area."

"I guess my night friend won't be able to come to me either," she said.

"It's for the safety of us all. We don't have much time left. I truly believe Troyington will kill the children and soon."

"I sent that same message to Raesheen." She gazed at him, trying to memorize him as he watched her. "You need to try to let me know what I can do to help and when you want me to do it."

"I'll try, but things are coming to a head. I don't know what's going to happen between today and tomorrow."

A bird's cry sounded overhead, and they both watched it fly over. "I know it hurts. Soon, it'll all be over, and we'll be together," he said. He ran down the path and disappeared into the trees.

She nodded, knowing nothing would come out of her mouth, even if she tried. She dragged herself toward Bradford's mansion. If she moved any faster than her current snail's pace, her heart just might shatter, taking her with it.

Chapter Twelve

"I don't understand how you got through that whole thing with Jack," Karen told Misty on the phone that night. "How did you keep your sanity with people hunting him and you every second?"

Misty snorted. "There were moments when I wasn't sure I'd make it." She paused. "Are you sure you're okay up there?"

Karen crossed to the window and stared at the night. She missed the guardian. "For now. The situation is a lot more complicated than I realized."

"Do you need the team? We'll be more than happy to bust some heads on your behalf."

Karen let the curtain fall back. "I'm not sure. There's innocent lives at stake. I shouldn't have even told you as much as I did."

The concern in Misty's voice deepened. "Okay. Let's back up a minute. What haven't you told me?"

"Everything," Karen whispered. "For the first time in my life, I'm truly afraid."

Silence. Then Misty asked, "Of what?"

Karen wiped at the tears that once again ran down her cheeks. She sniffed hard. "This whole situation."

"Are you crying?" She heard the disbelief in Misty's voice. "You never cry. You're the only one on the team that thinks with a clear head because you've got all your emotions under control."

Karen cleared her throat. "Things have changed. *I've* changed." She stopped talking and closed her eyes. "Misty, Randall's my soul mate."

"Ha!" Misty barked out. "I knew it."

Karen sank down on the bed. "But we can't be together here. And this other situation is making it almost impossible to talk to him." She stared at the floor. "This is so hard."

"We can be there in an hour," Misty said.

Karen paused. Would it be dangerous to bring in her team? Maybe. Maybe not. "I could use your help. But you'd better get here sometime tomorrow. It's getting late, and the roads up here are really narrow. Better to come in the daylight when you can see." She shook her head. "I didn't mean to worry you. I just wish Randall and I could be together."

"It's okay," Misty said. "Now, what's keeping you apart?"

"Bradford's threatened us," she said simply.

"I'm getting the car right now."

Karen listened to the determination in Misty's voice. Maybe this was just what she needed. Knowing her friends had her back would definitely help her frame of mind. "Not now, please. When you guys get here tomorrow, stay at the little town down the hill. It's not too far from the estate. I don't want Bradford knowing you're here. Can you make sure Rena comes with you? I think a telepath would be helpful."

Misty chuckled. "Are you kidding? Rena never passes up an opportunity to kick butt and take names."

"I thought as much." Karen smiled as Dayla appeared on her pillow. "And when you guys get here, you can join the army I have gathering."

"An army?" Misty sounded surprised. "Of who?"

Karen smiled, giving Dayla a thumbs up. "Would you believe, fairies?"

****

Karen made sure the ruby necklace was fastened securely around her neck as she made her way down to dinner. She fingered it and muttered, "How can something so delicate feel like such a lead weight?"

Bradford rose as she entered the dining room. "So, have you forgiven me yet?"

She returned his smile. The whole situation was comical, questions asked more out of routine than concern. "Only if you've forgiven me."

Moving to her usual place, she nodded at Edna. "I assume you've heard about our disagreement?"

Edna nodded, watching her every move as she sat. "Yes. There are bound to be a few rough spots as you two get used to each other."

Karen glanced at the two of them, noticing the little looks they exchanged. *They don't trust me. Fine. The feeling's mutual.*

Karen laid her napkin in her lap. "You said you've got a way to keep Randall away from me. Mind sharing?"

Bradford sat back, his gaze shifting between the two women. Edna's face said she knew what he was planning. "I've decided to show you tomorrow."

She frowned. "Why can't you tell me now?"

"I'm still working out some bugs." He turned that same cold, mirthless smile to her he had the day before. "Don't worry. I think you'll be impressed with my solution."

Karen's stomach grew cold, and her legs shook

under the table. Impressed? Horrified was probably going to be closer to the truth. What did he mean?

She sipped her water. *What am I up against?*

****

Karen and Bradford sat on the loveseat after dinner, watching the fire crackle merrily, trying to dispel the tension in the room.

Bradford stared at the flames. "You never did deny your feelings for Dupré," he said flatly.

She sat up, staring at him. "Why is this so important?"

"Why do you continue to evade it?" he said, never moving. "I could've given you anything and everything you could ever want. Yet, you pick that freak."

She laid her hand on his arm. "Didn't we just go through this earlier today? I'm with you all the time."

He faced her, his eyes almost sad, and laid his hand on her cheek. "And still, you don't say it. I could've loved you. There's a power in you that calls to me, but your unwillingness to deny Dupré tells me all I need to know."

Her face burned where his hand touched her. "And what's that?"

"You're in love with him." He dropped his hand, turning back to watch the fire. "This changes everything, all my plans, absolutely everything."

"I'm so sorry, Bradford," she said, her voice quiet. "I never wanted to hurt you."

"Don't say anything else," he murmured. "Please go to your room. I need to think."

Karen went to the door of the library. He sounded so lonely, so hurt, she almost felt sorry for him, but then she remembered his cruelty to Randall and the children.

Night Angel

"I'll see you in the morning."

"Yes," he said, his eyes boring into her. "You will."

Karen trembled as she climbed the main staircase and hurried to her room, his last words echoing in her ears. What did he mean? They certainly weren't said to comfort her. She threw her suitcase on the bed. She'd meet the other Angels in the town. As long as Bradford needed Randall, her soul mate was safe. But she needed to get the hell out of there while she could.

A quiet click behind her snapped her around to face the door. She tiptoed over and twisted the handle. So much for that idea. Bradford had her locked in. Well, she'd just go around the balcony to another room. Not a problem. She flung open the french doors, determined to leave.

Karen stared at the tree where the guardian had sat and talked with her. She plucked a leaf off and twirled it between her fingers, wishing he were there. Loneliness threatened to consume her.

"I wanted to tell you I'm leaving this house," she whispered. "I'll still be nearby to help you save the children, but I've got to get out of here."

Nothing. No rustling of leaves, no fluttering of wings, no sound at all. She closed her eyes wanting him or Randall to appear in front of her.

Funny how the guardian disappeared when Randall was also nowhere to be found. But they did agree that he wouldn't be coming to her anymore. But why wasn't the guardian to be found during the day? Where was Randall at night?

Her thoughts circled around to her earlier suspicions. If Randall was the guardian, it would explain a lot. He seemed to know every word she and the guardian spoke. The same was true of the guardian. He knew every detail of what happened between her and Randall. Magic or not, fairy or not, nobody remembered every tiny detail. And everyone addressed Randall as "guardian."

She took several steps to her right. A blackbird landed in front of her, its laughing call mocking her thoughts and feelings. It sidestepped closer, its beady black eyes watching her closely. She turned in the other direction and two more landed, staring at her with their unblinking eyes. More joined their kin as Karen backed away slowly, her eyes never leaving them.

Dayla appeared next to her head, tugging on her hair. "Come inside, miss, quickly."

Karen stepped over her threshold and closed and locked the doors. "So much for getting the heck out of here," she muttered. "Don't they ever take a break?" She pulled out her cell phone, frowning when she saw the battery was missing. She tried contacting Rena through the telepathic link all the Angels shared, but couldn't seem to break through. *I knew Jeffries was a psionic. It really just figures.*

"They can't. Not as long as Harmon's power influences them." Dayla peeked out the curtain, shuddering at the amount of birds on the balcony. "I wish we could get through to them. They don't think they're doing anything bad, and that's why we can't break his hold on them. They like him." Dayla frowned. "They think he's their friend."

Karen shook her head. If the wood folk couldn't free the animals, it would make their situation even more dire than it was right now. She took a last look at the birds and held her hand out, letting Dayla settle there. "I need some information, and please, tell me the truth."

Dayla crossed her heart. "I will answer you as truthfully as possible. Fairy's honor."

Karen took a deep breath. "Can the bonds between me and Randall be broken?"

Dayla chewed her lip. "Yes."

Karen sat down at the desk, letting Dayla climb from her hand. "If I say I don't believe in any of you, that I don't believe in magic, will I lose all of you?"

Dayla's head bobbed up and down. "Yes." She leaned on Karen's hand. "You haven't done that, have you?" She frowned. "You couldn't have, otherwise I wouldn't be here."

"No. I've minded my words." Karen sat back, drumming her fingers. "Bradford keeps trying to make me deny Randall and I had to convince him I didn't believe in fairies or magic without actually saying it." She rubbed her eyes. "This is getting way too complicated."

"You're doing well, miss," Dayla said. "I don't know many people who could've kept their wits about them like you've done."

"Comes from being a superhero," she muttered. Karen studied the fairy. "Are Randall and the guardian the same person?"

"That's one question I can't answer," Dayla said in a low voice. "I've made a promise to someone else to not say anything about the guardian."

Dayla's answer seemed to confirm what she suspected. She sighed. Why couldn't the guardian be here to give her the answers she needed? She was getting impatient with not having any success with anything she was trying to do or find out.

She slammed her fist into her palm. "I just want to kick their butts and make them tell me where the kids are. I'm tired of playing their games."

Dayla's face turned serious. "I don't think that's such a good idea."

"I was kidding," Karen said. Then she grinned. "For now."

Dayla grinned back. "I want to be with you when you do your butt-kicking thing."

Karen laid out her nightshirt and sweatpants. "Of course. I'll need you and anyone else you can bring with you, and my friends are coming. You ain't seen nothing yet, my tiny friend."

Dayla gave her a snappy salute. "Your fairy army will be ready when you give the word, miss. We'll make a great team."

Karen tugged her nightshirt over her head. "That's what I'm hoping."

Peeking out the window, she counted at least twenty blackbirds sitting outside her door, watching her. She shivered, pulling the curtains closer together. There was something unnerving about the way they just watched and called out with their laughing voices.

"I don't think tomorrow's going to be a very good day," she murmured. She lifted the fairy to her face. "If you can, find the guardian and tell him I miss him and Randall. I need them both."

"I will, miss." Dayla hugged Karen's nose. "Good night. Be well."

Karen watched Dayla scoot under the door. She felt lonelier than ever without the fairy's presence. She threw the covers back on the bed, crawling between the soft sheets, and turned out the bedside lamp with a loud click.

She lay there, watching the shadows dance across the ceiling. The birds outside flapped their wings, the rustling of their feathers loud in the darkness. Her heart pounded as she watched the silhouettes pace back and forth. The glass seemed too thin to stand between her and the flock on the balcony. She rolled over, unable to stand watching them any longer.

She thought about Bradford. He knew everything. What did he have planned? And did she really want to know? Her brain shifted into overdrive as she conjured up all sorts of horrible scenarios. Had he hurt Randall or the guardian? Would he hurt her?

She sat up, punching her pillow with a little more force than necessary. She settled back down, wishing Randall were next to her. Was he safe? Was he thinking about her? Could Dayla get her message to him?

Her eyes drifted shut. One way or another, tomorrow she'd have her answers.

Chapter Thirteen

The cheeriness of the morning sun was in direct contrast to Karen's mood as she dressed and brushed out her hair. The birds still sat on the balcony, their black eyes watching her every move.

She breathed a sigh of relief when Dayla appeared on the dresser. "Good morning, Dayla." She extended her hand, letting the fairy climb on.

Dayla sat cross-legged on Karen's hand. "I worried about you all night, miss. Raesheen thinks you're in danger."

Karen walked to the bed, and Dayla hopped off her hand when she grabbed her shoes. "I can handle Bradford and his men." She turned to the fairy. "Did you find Randall or the guardian?"

Dayla paced on the bed, her hands clasped behind her back. "No one has seen either one of them since yesterday."

Karen's chest tightened. She wrapped her arms around herself, trying to ward off the internal chill pushing its way up to her skin. "Bradford said he had a plan to keep us apart. You don't think..."

Images of Randall, broken and bleeding, filled her mind's eye, making her heart nearly stop. She closed her eyes, willing the repulsive vision away as cold sweat trickled down her spine.

Dayla shook her head. "No. We would've felt it,

and you would've definitely known."

Karen's shoulders sagged with relief. "But what could've happened to him?"

The fairy shrugged. "I've never understood how mere humans can be so good at hiding people. Especially people like me."

The click of the lock had Karen jumping to her feet as Dayla disappeared. Jeffries stood there, looking down his nose at her. She stepped back from the menace in his silent stance as he glared at her.

"Mr. Troyington requests you to come down for breakfast. Now." He moved to the side, indicating she should go first.

Karen pressed her back to the door and inched by him, not wanting to touch him. For good or ill, this was it. Bradford and Edna were already seated as she arrived. She watched the two of them as they stared at her, and again, that large chunk of ice moved into her stomach to sit there, freezing her soul. She took a deep, shaky breath and walked into the room.

"Good morning," she said, surprised she could keep the tremor from her voice.

Bradford waited as she settled herself at the table. "I've decided to show you my private study this morning." His face betrayed no emotion, no hint of what he had planned. He glanced at Edna, nodding slightly at her.

Karen's eyes widened. "Really? I didn't expect you to, seeing as how we're having some issues between us right now."

Bradford poured them all some coffee. "I know things are a bit strained, but I think this will help put everything into perspective." He sat back, a small smile finally coming out.

Not good, her combat instincts screamed. "What kind of perspective?"

He chewed silently for a few minutes, watching her face. "I've got something in there that will be of particular interest to you."

I doubt that. She turned to Edna. "Do you know what's in there?"

The older woman's mouth curled up in a sneer. "Of course."

Karen laid her fork down. The few bites she'd eaten churned in her stomach, making nausea rise and fall in her throat. Her hands trembled as she laid her napkin on the table. "Let's go now. I'm not very hungry."

Bradford practically jumped to his feet. "Excellent. I didn't want to wait any longer."

He grabbed her wrist, pulling her along to his study. He unlocked the door, shut down the security system, and lightly pushed her inside. He flipped on the light switch, watching her face as she looked around. She heard Edna shut the door and lock it.

The low light cast strange shadows into the corners. The study was smaller than Karen thought it would be. It was plain with just a desk and two chairs in front, a small bookcase, and a few filing cabinets. The wall to her right was empty of everything. No pictures, no furniture, nothing. She stared at the plain wall and her body trembled.

Karen glanced around the small room. "I don't know what I expected, but it wasn't this."

Bradford picked up a remote and turned to her. "This is only part of the room. I have a separate room that joins this one. Edna conducts a lot of her experiments there."

Karen turned to Edna. "I didn't know you where a scientist," she lied.

Edna eyed her, and Karen felt her skin crawl under the older woman's watchful stare. "Geneticist."

Mad scientist is more like it.

Bradford perched on the corner of his desk. "Edna is in the middle of something big and on the verge of a major breakthrough."

He gestured she should sit down in one of the chairs. "You wanted to see my office. Well, here it is." He opened his arms wide, indicating the small room. "What do you think?"

"It's very private," she said, feeling he wanted her to say something.

Edna moved to stand behind her. "Bradford and I have been talking about you. I convinced him this was the best course of action to take. He wasn't too sure, but I reminded him that you know about too many things around here."

He flipped the remote in his hand. "And the best is yet to come."

Karen turned and shrank back from the maniacal look on Edna's face. "What do you mean?"

Edna placed her hands on Karen's shoulders, holding her in the chair. "Tell her."

Bradford folded his hands in his lap and leaned forward. "I know about the nightly visits you've had from the guardian."

Karen frowned and tried to rise from the chair. Edna's grip on her tightened. She was stronger than Karen would've thought for an older woman. "That's ridiculous."

"Is it?" The look on his face said he didn't believe her. "When you arrived here, I'd hoped we'd share the same vision, the same ideas." His eyes narrowed. "But the longer you're here, the more you stink of fairy magic. However, I'm going to give you one more chance."

Karen's instincts started screaming to take them out and run. But she couldn't. Not until she found out what had happened to Randall. "A chance for what?"

He pointed the remote at the wall, pressing a button and it slid silently upwards. "Let me show you."

Bright fluorescent light flooded the room, making Karen blink several times as her eyes adjusted. Randall faced off with Cray while Harmon stood off to the side, holding a knife to a teen girl's throat. Randall blocked a blow from Cray and crashed back into the glass, streaking it with blood and making it shudder.

"What are you doing?" Karen tried again to rise, but Edna still held her down. "Stop it, Bradford! I mean it!"

He laughed, a dark mirthless sound that made Karen's body shake harder. "You don't like the game?" He grabbed her left arm while Edna held her right as they led her to the window. "If Dupré hurts Cray, Harmon cuts the girl's throat with a silver dagger. No regenerating from that, right, Edna?"

Edna nodded eagerly. "Right."

"If he does nothing, Cray will break him in two and I'll be rid of him. Either way I win."

He rapped on the glass, getting Cray's attention. He gestured for Randall to be brought to the window. Cray yanked Randall to his feet and shoved his head against the glass. Bradford pushed Karen closer.

Karen could see the cuts and bruises on Randall's face and arms from the beating he'd sustained at Cray's hands. He stared at her and she lifted a hand to the glass. He raised his gaze to Bradford and Karen could see in his face he knew what was coming.

Bradford pushed a second button on the small remote and she could hear Randall's ragged breathing and the girl's quiet sobbing. Bradford leaned close and whispered, "Deny him. Say it and all will be forgiven between us. Stay silent and I'll kill them both right now as you watch."

Karen watched Cray heft a metal bar in his hands. Randall wouldn't survive a blow from that, not in his present condition. And the girl was innocent. She looked in his eyes, those eyes that reminded her of ice on fire. He nodded, knowing what she had to do.

"I deny him," she whispered.

Bradford laid a hand to his ear. "What was that? I couldn't quite hear you."

Karen took a deep breath, hot tears scalding her face as she stared into Randall's eyes, watching her words hurt him more deeply than Cray ever could. "I deny him," she said louder.

Randall's eyes closed and his head dropped as her words reached him. He sank to his knees as Cray laughed, and Karen balled her hands, longing to go through the glass and wipe the smug look off his face.

Bradford gave her a sharp shake. "Say it one more time and the bonds will be broken for all time."

Break his heart, save his life. Karen hated Bradford more than anyone in her life. She wanted to hold Randall, to comfort him and make everything all right.

But she'd just been forced to destroy any future they would've had together. Break his heart. Save his life. She followed him down to the floor, wanting to stay beside him as long as possible.

"I deny him."

Bradford yanked her to her feet. "Get him up, Cray. I want him to see this."

He grabbed Karen and kissed her as Randall watched. He turned her to the glass and opened the top few buttons on her shirt. "This is mine now. You'll never know what it's like to have her."

"How does 'no' grab you?" Karen growled.

She rammed her elbow straight back, catching him in the stomach. His breath whooshed out of him, and he stumbled back as she spun around, catching him with an open palm strike. He fell to the floor, surprise and rage competing for dominance on his face.

Karen shoved Edna to one side, running for the door. She opened the lock she'd heard Edna set when Bradford grabbed her shoulders and shoved her toward the desk. She spun with a roundhouse kick to his head. He fell to the floor, and Karen grabbed a fistful of his jacket. "Randall, the girl, and I are leaving now. You'd be smart to let us."

"I don't think so," Edna said behind her.

A sharp pin prick stabbed the back of her neck. She slapped at it, turning to see the older woman with an empty hypodermic needle in her hand. Karen staggered, grabbing the back of the chair. She blinked, her vision blurring badly. She heard someone shouting her name from far away and turned her head to see Randall pounding on the glass.

Bradford stood, straightening his clothes. He

rubbed his head where her foot had connected. "Thank you, Edna." He looked at Karen. "I was expecting you to try something like that, so I told Edna to be prepared. Don't worry. She injected you with a mild sedative. It'll wear off soon."

Karen sank to the floor as she tried to get her legs to take her to Randall. As her hand touched the glass, her world went black.

****

She was cold. Karen squeezed her eyes shut tighter, then opened them slowly. She was lying on a concrete floor. She sat up, massaging her temples to get her brain functioning again and her mouth felt stuffed with cotton. A water bottle sat next to her on the floor and she grabbed it, drinking half without stopping.

A hand reached out, pulling the bottle away from her mouth. "Not too much at once. You'll make yourself sick."

She looked up, trying to make her eyes focus. "Randall?" She grabbed his arm. "Are you all right?"

He smiled, kneeling beside her. "I should be asking you that."

She grabbed a fistful of his T-shirt. "The girl that was with you. What about her?"

"Nikki's fine," he said, then grinned. "Do you always worry about everyone but yourself?"

Her heart flip-flopped in her chest. "Yes." She threw her arms around him. "I'm so sorry. I didn't want to deny you, but Bradford gave me no choice. I'm so sorry I caused you pain."

Randall wrapped his arms around her. "You didn't," he whispered.

She sat back, watching his eyes sparkle with

amusement at her confusion. "But Bradford said..."

He laid a finger on her lips. "Do you remember what the guardian told you about the power of names?"

She nodded, wondering where he was going with this line of thought.

"By not saying my name when you denied me, the bonds stayed intact. As far as the magic knows, you could've been denying broccoli."

She raised an eyebrow. "Broccoli? Really?"

He grinned wider, shaking his head. "Not really. But you didn't say my name, so it didn't work. That's all that matters."

"For now," Bradford said from the doorway, Cray and Harmon behind him. "Didn't you think I'd be able to tell if it worked or not? I sense things like that."

Randall shot to his feet and stood in front of Karen. "You won't touch her again, Troyington. I won't let you hurt her."

Bradford folded his arms and chuckled. "Why should I want to hurt her? I'm going to let you do it for me." He stared at them. "I thought having her break the bonds was the best thing to do at the time. Then, when I felt everything still intact, I came up with this solution and I like it much better."

Randall frowned. "What do you mean?"

Bradford smiled that evil sneer again. "You're a smart boy. Figure it out."

Karen stood next to Randall. She'd seen a lot of emotions cross his face, but this was the first time he looked panicked. "What's wrong?"

He didn't answer, just took several steps toward the door.

Karen's hands shook as he remained quiet. "You

know what he's planning, don't you?"

Randall nodded. "He's going to keep us locked in here all night."

Bradford clapped. "Very good, Dupré. I know about your nightly visits and what you haven't shown her, so I thought this would be the perfect opportunity for you."

Karen looked back and forth between the two of them. Dread crawled through her as she watched fear fill Randall's face and the overconfidence in Bradford's. She opened her mouth to ask Randall to explain, but the words jammed in her throat.

"When the sun sets in—" Bradford looked at his watch. "—nine hours and twenty-two minutes, all will become clear." He motioned for Cray and Harmon to leave. "When you finally see what a monster he really is, you'll be begging me to take you back." He paused at the door. "But I won't. I'm done with you, both of you. See you in the morning, Ms. Spraiker."

The door slammed shut, the boom echoing through the room.

Chapter Fourteen

Randall ran toward the door, slamming his fist against it and cried out as the metal seared his flesh. There was a loud click as they were sealed in. "Troyington, no! Don't do this to her!"

He hung his head, squeezing his eyes shut. "Please," he said in a low voice. "Don't do this."

Karen pushed on the locked door. "Well, it's not opening this time." She stared at the claw marks on the walls to either side of the door, dried blood coloring the set to her right a dark brown. She ran her fingers over them. "Edna tried to explain these away but something wasn't happy about being here."

Randall rubbed his hand where it connected with the door. "It was me," he mumbled.

Karen turned sharply to stare at him. "What?"

She thought about the guardian's hand and those long claws and touched the marks lightly. Karen smiled a little as the pieces fell together and formed the puzzle she knew it would. She figured right. Randall was the guardian who came to her at night.

"Nothing." He lifted his head, staring at her. "We don't have much time left. I need you to do something for me."

Karen hurried to him, watching him watch her. "Tell me. I'd do anything for you."

He lifted his hands to her face and held her. "Just

Night Angel

remember right now, at this point in time, you loved me." He gathered her into his arms, holding her tight.

She rested her head against his chest and closed her eyes. "Wait a minute." She stood back. "Is something going to happen to make me stop loving you?"

He kissed her forehead. "In a few hours, everything's going to change." He looked away. "I'm afraid."

"Of what?" she asked, trembling as his fear bled into her.

"Of losing you," he whispered. "When you see who I truly am."

"You won't," she said firmly, trying to make him believe it. "I promise."

Fire crept its way back to his eyes as his fingers glided down her neck. He kissed her, his tongue tasting and teasing, pulling a passion from her she didn't know she had. "Remember you said that."

She could feel his power rise around her, but it felt different. Instead of warming her, it ignited her, raising a blinding silver light behind her eyes. She squirmed in his arms, trying to relieve the pressure building inside.

"My skin feels too tight and I'm seeing light," she panted.

"Your power's trying to merge with mine," he whispered against her lips, holding her tighter. "Let it. By keeping your emotions in check, you've chained it. Set it free."

Her body shook from the energies pushing against her, inside and out. "I don't know how."

He lowered her shirt off her shoulder, trailing kisses along her neck. "You carry the dragon spirit in you. Just picture it rising and it will. Focus. Control it."

Karen gripped his arms, the contact giving her the confidence she needed to release the power coiled inside. Closing her eyes, she saw her power as a long, sinewy Chinese dragon. Randall's power guided her, leading her on a path through her own psyche to the silver light at her core.

As she pictured it rising, it burst free from the invisible bonds holding it in place. She opened her eyes to see the silver dragon curl around a strange lavender creature with large wings. The two energies flowed around each other, looking like they were playing before becoming one and pouring into the couple who summoned them.

He laid a shaking hand over her heart. "I pictured this happening from the first moment I saw you." He traced a finger up to her collar bone. "I can feel your power in me. I've never sensed anything this strong."

She smiled at Randall, trying to quell the sadness in his eyes. "There's no one stopping you now. And any power I have, it's all yours."

He closed his eyes, bowing his head. "Don't say that. Not until tomorrow."

She slipped her hands under his shirt and ran them over his chest. "I'm not sure what you're afraid of, but it'll be all right." She looked down. "Why are you always barefoot?"

He smiled as he knelt in front of her, removing her shoes and socks. "It's part of who I am. Try it."

She returned his smile, desire jumping in her veins as the cold from the concrete floor seeped into the soles of her feet. "Let's try being barefoot all over."

Randall unhooked her jeans, pushing them and her panties down together. He slowly stood, running his hands up her legs. He unbuttoned her shirt, letting it fall from her shoulders, her bra following. "You've got goose bumps."

Yanking his T-shirt over his head, Karen ran her hands across his chest, sighing at the warmth flowing from him. "You're always so warm. I don't think I'll have goose bumps for long." She pushed his pants off his hips.

"Do you remember that morning in the clearing?" he asked, his voice deepening. "Let me show you what was supposed to happen at the end."

He took her hand, turning her back to him and pulled her tight against his chest. "Remember the music," he whispered, his breath tickling her ear and sending shivers through her. "It's part of you now. You can pull it forth whenever you want. Hear it. Let the rhythm move your body."

She nodded and closed her eyes, hearing the music deep inside. Randall guided her feet through the intricate steps of the dance as his hand rested on her bare stomach. Karen felt every hair on her body stand up from the electricity of his touch. She laid her head back on his shoulder, the cool air whispering over her naked body, making the dance feel more sensual, more arousing than it had before.

His face was rough with stubble as she rubbed her cheek to his. Karen reached back, her hand lying on the back of his neck, his hair brushing her knuckles. Their hips pressed together as their feet moved, weaving the age-old pattern. She took a deep breath, inhaling the strange, exotic smell of the magic around them.

She pushed closer to him as they moved in time to the remembered song, the feel of his skin jolting her harder than it had the first the time. The power in her thrummed as the song built to its crescendo, getting brighter and brighter until she thought her body would explode from the heat and light pouring from it.

Randall held her hand as she spun away, then back. He bowed to her, raising her hand to his lips. He let his hand glide up her arm to her neck, and he pulled her close, igniting the passion within her, allowing her power fill him, pouring his into her. His calloused fingers were gentle as they whispered just above her skin. This time, as the dance ended, he pulled her close and they shared the kiss that bonded them together as soul mates.

"We were meant for each other, Karen." He dropped his head to her shoulder, his lips trailing fire along her neck. "Can you feel it?"

She nodded. "Yes." She took a deep breath then slowly released it. "But I need you now. We've waited too long for this moment."

"Don't rush things," he murmured, his lips just brushing her neck. "It'll happen just the way it should."

Her legs trembled as she tried to meld her body with his. She slid her arms around his neck and pulled his face closer to hers. "We both need this, if for nothing else to anchor each other."

His smile faded and he looked away, just for a moment. Something changed in him as sadness replaced the fire his eyes. He laid her on their clothes and pressed a light kiss between her breasts.

He brushed his knuckles along her cheek. "I'm sorry this isn't more romantic. I didn't picture our first time together being in a concrete cell."

Threading her fingers through his midnight hair,

she stared into his magical eyes. "I don't care. As long as I'm with you."

He lightly ran his fingers over her body, his gaze following. She could almost see him trying to memorize every line, every curve of her body. He laid his hand on her stomach, then moved down to gently touch her folds. She opened her legs, inviting him to take what she offered. His fingers slid over and in her. She let her own hand move down to find him and hold him tenderly, making him groan.

She shivered, not from the cool air in the room, but from the fear she sensed in him hanging on. "Don't be afraid," she whispered. "We both know this was meant to be."

He gazed in her eyes. "I know. I just don't want to disappoint you."

"You could never do that," she whispered. Letting him go, she ran her hands up his arms to stroke his chest, smiling when she felt him tremble. "Right now, no fear, no doubt. Just you and me."

Randall nodded before pulling her breast into his mouth, her back arching with pleasure. She jumped as his fingers probed more deeply inside her, making her writhe beneath his hands. He smiled as she opened herself completely, pulling him over her.

Karen wrapped her legs around him, giving him no choice as she held him tight. As he slowly entered her, she watched his eyes turn from the pale-blue ice that captivated her, to deep, blue flame, searing her with the wild magic flowing inside him. She grasped his shoulders, feeling him tremble beneath her fingers.

Light flared around them, bringing a sense of urgency to their passion, glowing bright as the sun. A glow exploded from both of them as they shook with the power of their climax. He smiled, wiping the single tear that rolled down her cheek.

Karen smiled, not wanting to let him go. "I never thought I'd ever experience anything so wonderful, so completely fulfilling." She felt his power flow through her. "It goes so far beyond the physical bond."

He kissed her lightly. "We're soul mates now, in the truest sense of the word. You've given me your power, your self." He grinned. "I didn't think you were supposed to cry, though."

She smiled, lightly slapping his chest. "Stop it. I've never felt anything like this before. I can *feel* your power in me."

He held her, laying her head on his chest. "All I want is to hold you, to love you forever." His gaze drifted toward the ceiling. "But there's one more obstacle to overcome, and I don't know if you'll want me then."

"What's left besides dealing with Bradford and his people?"

"You'll see at sunset." He stood, pulling her to her feet. "Troyington will be back to taunt us some more. You don't want him finding you like that."

"Just one more kiss," she said.

He bent his head to hers, stopping just above her lips so his breath warmed them. She closed the space between them, drawing a sharp breath when her body brushed his. Randall ran his hands across her breasts, making her body respond faster than it had before. "Do you know what you do to me?"

She smiled and glanced down. He was ready to go again. "I have a pretty good idea."

"I wish we had more time," he said, pulling her close. "But we don't, and we need to be ready when they return."

She nodded and pulled on her clothes, wondering what would happen when the sun went down.

****

They sat on the floor, leaning against the wall. Randall said nothing, just held her, occasionally placing small kisses on her forehead. Fear still filled his eyes. If only he'd tell her what the problem was, she could help. She'd understand.

The lock clicked, shooting them to their feet. The door swung wide, and Troyington and his men entered.

"It's almost sunset," Troyington said, looking at his watch.

Randall glared at him, hate blazing from his eyes. "You think I don't know that?"

Troyington walked over to Karen, his nose wrinkling. "You reek of fairy magic, and now we have the underlying scent of sex. What was it like, mating with an animal?"

Karen pulled herself up to her full height. "I don't know. You never had a chance to touch me."

He laughed, making her take a step back. "Very good. I wouldn't have expected anything less from you." He turned to Randall. "I wish I could be here when the sun sets, but I have things to do, and I'm done wasting my time with you."

Randall just stared at him, a scowl darkening his face. Karen watched his hands ball and knew what he was thinking. His power burned hot inside her, making her own flare in response. Cray moved to strike him, and Randall's arm shot out with a speed she'd never seen, forcing the other man's arm down. "Don't even think about it," he growled, his voice deep, rich, and full of anger.

Troyington and his men stepped back into the hall. "You two have a good night."

After the door was locked again, Karen started to walk to Randall but stopped short when he threw his hand up. "Stay back. The sun is setting." He pulled off his clothes, throwing them in the corner.

He turned his back to her. Her eyes widened as she watched two large lumps grow on each shoulder blade, and one form at the base of his spine. Two huge dragon-like wings burst from his back, fanning to either side of him, glistening from their nightly birth. A thick, leathery tail stretched from his spine to grow and lay behind him on the floor. Karen backed up, watching the appendage flip around in agitation.

His legs lengthened and widened as new muscles formed. His skin rippled, bones popping and cracking as they changed to resemble an animal's back legs, claws sprouting from his toes, his skin darkening to a rich purple. He straightened, rising far above his human height to over seven feet. His arms thickened and his shoulders broadened to support the wings on his back. Claws extended from his fingers as the change continued. His hair grew longer, flowing down his back in an ebony wave between his wings and stopping just above his tail.

He turned to her, his face elongated just enough to distort his human features. His brow protruded over his eyes, the only part of him that hadn't changed. They stared at her, sadness filling them as he watched her back away from him.

He pulled himself up to his full height. "See me, Karen, as I am in the night."

His voice rumbled through her. Here was her night visitor. His naked body still magnificent, even though he was no longer human. His power sang in her, making her own answer with a surge she wouldn't have expected.

She could feel the fairy magic hum around them, filling her up to the point where she thought she'd burst. Her vision grew sharper as the earth called to her. She wanted to dance with sudden joy as a feeling of welcome wrapped around her. The night sang in her veins as Randall's power changed with his body. This, she knew, was what was exactly meant to be for them.

"You're taller than I thought you'd be. What exactly are you?"

He took a step toward her. "I'm a human/gargoyle hybrid. By day, I'm Randall Dupré. At sundown, I become a guardian, protector of the fairy realm."

Karen watched him take a few steps in her direction. "I should be really mad at you right now."

He stopped. "I know."

"Not for the reason you were so afraid of." She smiled as his gaze shot to her face. "Troyington was right. I *am* a great detective."

He frowned. "I don't understand."

She chuckled. "I figured out you were the guardian awhile ago. It just kills me I have to admit Troyington was right about something."

"You're not mad at me?"

She grinned. "I should be, considering you'd think I'd turn from you because at night you grow wings and turn purple. This isn't even close to some of the things

I've seen as a hero. I'd never leave you, Randall." She let her gaze roam over his body. "Besides, no matter what form you're in, you look really good naked."

He smiled as he held his arms open and she ran to him. She held him tightly as his wings folded around them. She snuggled closer, letting the warmth of his body comfort her as she drifted off to sleep.

Chapter Fifteen

Karen blinked the sleep from her eyes and looked up to see Randall extending his hand to her. He was wide awake and dressed. He pulled her to her feet and she rocked her head from side to side, rubbing the back of her neck. "You're really comfortable for a rock, but I shouldn't have slept in one position all night."

He turned her around, gently massaging her neck and shoulders. "Better?"

"Yes." She turned in his arms. "I wish we had more time. I'd like to try that whole bonding thing again."

Randall smiled and pulled her closer. "I know what you mean."

She smoothed his hair off his forehead. "I want you to promise me something."

"Anything."

She gazed into his eyes. "I don't want you to be afraid of telling me anything ever again. I'm your soul mate. I'll always stand by you."

Randall leaned closer to her. "I promise. Anything you want to know, I'll tell you."

"Good," she whispered before brushing his lips with hers.

The locked clicked, and Randall moved in front of Karen as Troyington and his men entered. He stood in the doorway for a moment, staring at the two of them.

A quick look of disbelief crossed his face, but then the familiar cold smile returned as he headed toward them.

"How was your night?"

Karen eyed him warily as he circled them. "It was all right but a little chilly. You should think about putting a heater in here. It would make the room a little more comfortable."

Troyington frowned. "The people put here aren't supposed to be comfortable."

Karen tapped her chin. "Oh, yes. People you're afraid of. People like Randall."

He grabbed her arm, making her wince. "Dupré is a freak of nature. You saw that for yourself. You should be begging me to take you back."

She yanked her arm from his grasp, stepping back to feel Randall's arms go around her waist. "He might not be human, but at least he's not you."

Troyington's face flushed a deep crimson and his eyes darkened. "Fine," he said, his voice shaking with anger. "If that's your choice, then his fate will be yours. I thought you would've had more sense than to choose a monster."

"I didn't," she retorted. "I chose Randall."

Troyington stormed out, his men behind him, slamming the door hard enough to make their ears ring. She sagged against Randall, feeling their power flare. She laid her head back and closed her eyes, seeing him the night before as the guardian, large and untouchable and deliciously naked.

Karen turned in his arms. "When we get out of this, I'm burning those pants."

His hands went to her hips and he pulled her close. "Oh? Why?"

She hooked her fingers in his waistband. "They've got this annoying habit of obscuring my view of you."

"I could say the same thing about yours." She felt her power protest as his pushed their desire down. "When we get out of here, I'll even light the match. But first, we have to get out."

She sighed. "Got it."

He led her to the door. "I can't get close enough to hear anything. Can you?"

She laid her ear against the door, jumping back as the metal shocked her. "Ow!" She rubbed her ear and scowled at the door. "That didn't happen yesterday."

Randall turned her head to see if she was burned. "Yesterday, you touched the door before we bonded. When we shared power, you took part of me inside you."

She winked. "More than one part."

He grinned. "The *power* part must've given you a partial vulnerability to cold iron."

"Maybe with the part of me you have, your vulnerability won't be so bad."

He eyed the door. "Let's see." He touched a finger to the door and jerked back with a yelp. He inspected his fingertip. It was red, but the blistering was almost nonexistent. It didn't even feel like a burn any more, but like tiny pin pricks.

He looked at Karen as he held up his hand for inspection. "I think your power gives me a little bit of protection. It still hurts and makes my skin crawl, but not as bad."

She held his hand, studying the burn. "There's no bubbles. I'm glad my power does something for you."

He gazed at her, curling his fingers around hers.

"Yes, it does."

She drew in a deep breath. "Stop looking at me like that, or we'll never get out of here." She leaned as close to the door as she dared. "I think I hear someone coming."

Karen stood next to Randall and steadied her breathing. She focused her combat sense, preparing for a fight. She could feel Randall's anger next her like a solid wall of granite. His power built inside her, darkening from light lavender to deep purple. She could almost taste his rage in her mouth. After so many years of keeping her emotions under control, she welcomed them and the strength they would give her.

Cray opened the door allowing Troyington to enter, followed by Edna and Harmon. He pushed the door shut and the group moved to confront them.

Troyington waved his men forward. "Hold him. He's not going to like what's going to happen."

Cray reached for Randall, and Karen's hand shot out, grabbing his arm. She bent his wrist at an unnatural angle. "Randall might not be able to fight you because of the contract you made him sign, but I'm not from his world. I can." She bent his wrist a little further, making him cry out. "You won't hurt him any more."

Troyington stepped closer to her. "But, my dear, we're here for you."

She looked at him. "I'm not going."

She jabbed Cray in the face with his own hand, knocking him to the floor. She threw a punch at Troyington, who blocked it easily. He blocked every punch from her in rapid succession, finally trapping her arms at her sides.

Randall grabbed Troyington around his neck from

behind. "Let her go." Troyington dropped his hold on Karen, and Randall threw him across the room.

Karen saw Cray surge to his feet, bringing his arm back to hit her. She crossed her arms in an X in front of her face. Pushing his fist out of the way, she hit his chest with an open palm strike. He staggered back, and she took him down with a low leg sweep.

Harmon grabbed Randall, throwing him against the concrete wall. Randall connected a solid punch to Harmon's chin before Harmon drove his meaty fist in to Randall's stomach, dropping him to the floor.

Karen faced off with Troyington when she felt an all too familiar stab at the back of her neck. Edna again stood behind her with an empty syringe.

Randall got to his knees as blood dripped from his head to the floor. "No!" Harmon grabbed his head and pushed him down before slamming him against the floor.

Karen blinked furiously trying to clear her vision. Troyington caught her as her legs gave out. She saw Randall lying unmoving on the floor, blood pooling under his head. His power dulled to a low light inside her, then nothing more.

****

Karen sat up, rubbed her head, and moaned. "I wish Edna would quit doing that."

"Quit what?"

She carefully turned her head and squinted to make out the figure of a teenage boy sitting next to her on the floor. "Stabbing me with needles to knock me out. It's getting old." She stuck her hand out. "I'm Karen. James, right?"

He shook her hand, eyeing her warily. "Right. How

do you know me?"

She stood up, taking a few wobbly steps as she brushed herself off. "I was there the day Edna took blood samples from you." She pulled him to his feet. "I'm so sorry you've been hurt."

He shrugged. "They haven't done anything too bad to us yet, but I've got a feeling that's about to change. The Oracle told us you'd be coming. She said, 'When the dragon angel comes, the end will be near.' I could smell the dragon power in you as soon as you got dumped here."

Karen trembled as James' words sank in. Had time run out? Was she going to be able to save the pack children? Could she get a message to the Angels? How was she going to let Randall know?

James's eyes narrowed and he leaned closer to her, inhaling deeply. "You smell like the guardian," he said, interrupting her thoughts.

"We're soul mates." Karen watched James. "He told me what you and the others are."

Suspicion filled his face. "And that doesn't frighten you?"

She shook her head. "No. One of my best friends is a shape-shifter, and my soul mate changes into a gargoyle at night. You guys are comparatively normal."

He looked skeptical. "You make it a point to hang out with supernatural creatures?"

Karen nodded. "You could say that. I'm a member of a team of paranormals."

"This team got a name?" he asked. "I mean, if you're a 'superhero,' don't all those teams have names?"

She nodded again. "Yes, they do. My team is the

Angels."

"That is so *cool!*" said an excited voice behind her. The girl had short brown hair, and she wore a shirt hanging loosely from her narrow shoulders, and her pants sagged around her tiny hips.

Karen noticed the bandage on the side of her neck. "Nikki, right?"

The teen nodded vigorously. "I follow everything you guys do. I wish there was more about you in the papers."

Karen checked the girl's wound. "I'm glad you weren't seriously hurt the other day."

Her joy immediately vanished. "The guardian was, and it's all our fault."

James stood behind her. "It's his job to protect us."

She whirled around to face him. "The guardian suffers so we won't be hurt."

"That's what the guardians are trained for," James said, his voice rising. "They're the protectors of our realm."

Nikki scowled at him, then dismissed him with a wave of her hand. "Whatever."

Karen thought maybe James was trying a little too hard to convince Nikki. "James, we're out of time. Troyington has plans to dissect some of you."

The color drained from Nikki's face. "What do we do?"

"We find a way out of here." Karen looked around. "Where are we, anyway?"

"A cabin in the hills," James said, his voice shaking. "We've checked it out. We're not leaving until they let us."

The cabin! Karen had found it and still had no idea

where it was located. "Maybe a fresh pair of eyes can find something, and the wood folk know about this cabin."

James shook his head. "The one they know about is a decoy. This one's farther up in the hills and hidden somehow."

The door crashed open and Cray and Harmon stood there.

Karen moved in front of the teens. "Go in the other room, guys. Stay there until I come for you. Understand?"

James nodded as he pushed Nikki into the back room. Karen faced the two men.

Cray curled his hands into large fists. "Mr. Troyington wants all the teenagers."

Karen stepped back with her right foot, resting her weight on it. "Too bad."

Harmon glared at her. "Your wishes make no difference to us. Stand aside."

"It's a funny thing about heroes." She sprang forward, throwing punches at Harmon, staggering him back, then turned to Cray. "We don't like kids being hurt. We frown even harder on them being dissected to give some greedy bastard more power."

Karen blocked Cray's wild swing, but her movements were sluggish from the drugs still running through her system. As she pulled her arm back, Harmon clouted her on the back of her head, and while she was reeling, spun her around to strike her.

Karen threw her arm up, but he clipped her chin before throwing her against the wall, stunning her for a second. She struggled to pull air into her lungs as she blocked his kick, before delivering one of her own.

Cray jumped in and drove his fist down, knocking her to the floor.

"Give up the brats," he growled.

Karen forced herself not to groan. Between Edna's drugs and the short pounding she'd taken, her body just wanted to stay on the floor. She lifted her head and glared at them. "No. And you can tell your boss his days of experimentation are over."

Cray stood over her. "Mr. Troyington isn't going to like this."

She pushed herself to her feet, using a hand to steady herself against the wall. "You think I give a damn what Troyington likes?" she growled. "Think again." Harmon took a step toward her and she snapped her head around to glare at him. "You want more? Bring it!"

Cray stopped Harmon before he reached her. "Dupré said the same thing about a week ago and look where that's got him." Cray gave her an evil smile. "He's not going to live out the day." He pushed Harmon outside and slammed the door in her face.

"No!" She stumbled to the door and sank to the floor. "Dayla, if you can hear me, keep him safe."

Chapter Sixteen

Troyington walked around Randall. "Cray and Harmon are bringing the older brats here. It's time to begin the internal exam."

Randall stared straight ahead, keeping the fear from his face. If Troyington and his goons got the kids, it meant he'd failed the pack and his clan. "Go to hell."

Troyington leaned closer. "I also told them to get rid of your soul mate. I thought she might be useful, but I was mistaken. Like you, she's more trouble than she's worth."

Karen's power sang within him, flaring briefly. Randall gave Troyington a small smile. "I think Karen took exception to your orders."

Troyington slammed his fist into Randall's head, knocking him to the floor, opening the recent gashes. As Randall wiped at the blood running down the side of his face, Troyington kicked him in the stomach, doubling him up.

Edna came in, carrying two vials. She gestured to Randall, groaning on the floor. "Are you done with him?"

Troyington smoothed his hair back. "Yes. He's got nothing left I need."

"I thought as much." She watched Randall as he pushed himself to his knees. "I need to get one more sample from him before disposal."

He kissed her cheek. "Take whatever you want. He won't need it where's he's going. Just be careful." He glanced again at Randall. "He's unpredictable."

"In the condition he's in right now, I don't think I have to worry." She pushed him toward the door. "Now scoot. I've got work to do."

Edna shut the door behind him and turned to Randall. "This whole procedure will go much smoother if you don't fight me. I don't want to sedate you."

Randall glared at her. "You'd better use whatever you've got, because if you don't, I'm going to kill you. That's a promise."

Edna made clucking sounds with her tongue. "That doesn't sound good at all. I suppose I should."

She pulled out a hypodermic needle and jabbed it into his arm. "Now, this won't knock you out. It'll just make you more compliant with my wishes." She patted his cheek. "It's time to get those reproductive samples."

He collapsed to the floor as his muscles gave out. Just great, he thought. Trapped in a room with a mad scientist pervert.

"Now, I want you to think of your woman, of how beautiful she is," Edna said, rolling him to his back. "Think of how much you want her."

Randall tried to think of anything but Karen, but whatever she'd shot him with channeled his thoughts in a more erotic direction. He felt her hands on his hips, slowly massaging them. His body felt like mud. It looked like whether he wanted to or not, he was going to give Edna the samples she wanted.

She smiled at him. "Doing this helps my test subject to relax. You really are quite the looker." She started rubbing his thighs. "It's a shame I can't keep you."

Randall scowled. "You're dead. You know that, right?" he said, his words slurred.

She still smiled at him as she unhooked his jeans and pulled them partway down his legs. "I don't think so." She eyed his crotch and smiled as she dragged her hand across his stomach. "You're almost ready." She turned, setting up the vials and test tubes she brought with her.

Randall closed his eyes and thought of Karen. He could see her clearly in his mind. *Karen, I need you so much right now.*

****

Karen checked the front door. "Who makes a door with no handle on the inside?" She'd already determined there wasn't a back door. The window panes were shatterproof glass with bars crossing each other on the outside. The walls were solid logs, the floor concrete. There was no fireplace and nothing to use as a weapon. James was right. They were here to stay.

She slammed her fist against the door. "I can't believe this stupid door has no handle, no lock, nothing!" She gave a short scream of frustration.

James came up behind her. "What now?"

Karen sat cross-legged on the floor. She hadn't lost her temper like that since she'd been a little girl. "I need to calm down. Give me a few minutes, and we'll start again."

James nodded. "Call me when you're ready."

Karen closed her eyes. *Randall, I need you with me so badly right now.* He was definitely still alive; his power burned within her. She gave a mental sigh of relief.

She thought she heard something and frowned. Rena, the team telepath, had taught them all how to open their minds to pick up people trying to communicate with them.

Randall? she called with her mind.

Karen.

She could sense the relief in him at finding her. *Are you all right?*

Not really. Strathmore's getting ready to do kinky and perverted things to me.

Karen seethed with anger. Edna had no right to heap more abuse on her soul mate. If she could only be with him. Protect him. *Use my power.*

His mental voice grew faint. *I don't know if I can. She drugged me with something. I can't stop the reaction to it.*

Her hands clenched. *I'll help you.*

Karen searched inside herself, finding the spark that was her power. Randall's lavender light swirled around the silver in a beautiful and strange dance. She called both forth, strengthening them with her will before shooting them down the telepathic link to him.

****

"I think we'll be able to get rid of these pants in another minute or two," Edna said. "I believe you're almost set for me to take my samples."

Randall's back arched as Karen's power slammed into him. He could feel it burn the drugs in his system to nothing in seconds. Her light soothed the pains in his body as the silver dragon coiled around him, protecting him. He sat up, smacking Edna's hands away. His body had healed faster than ever. *Thanks, sweetheart.*

Edna quickly stood and ran for the door. Randall caught her, jerking her back to the center of the room.

"You know about my people," he said in a low voice. "I promised you were dead."

She backed away from him, terror on her face. "Stay away from me!"

"I'm bound by my word." He grabbed her arm. "No more experiments, doctor. No more anything." He twisted her head around with a sickening pop, dropping her lifeless body to the ground.

He closed his eyes as he knelt beside her, saying a silent prayer for her soul.

Randall stood and watched silver light dance across his body. He went to the cold iron door, and taking a deep breath, pushed it open. He hardly felt the metal sting his skin. He ran down the hallway, checking his hands. No burns, no blisters, nothing. Her power had saved him again. The silver light began to fade.

Karen? he called telepathically. He couldn't find her with his mind, but her power was still with him. He'd know if she'd been hurt. She must've exhausted herself.

He only had a few more hours until sundown. Then the search could truly begin.

****

Karen slumped forward as she felt the power return. She couldn't hear Randall's thoughts any more. "I don't know how Rena does it," she muttered. She wiped sweat from her forehead. It had taken more energy than she thought to maintain a telepathic link.

Nikki poked her head into the room. "Are you all right, Angel?"

Karen pushed herself to her feet. "Yeah. Just tired."

"I saw the dragon energy form around you. You're Sterling Dragon, aren't you?"

Karen smiled at her. "Guilty as charged." She stretched, working out some of the kinks from her neck and shoulders. Her body trembled as she remembered the feel of Randall's hands massaging her neck from that morning.

She closed her eyes, almost feeling the warmth of his hands on her skin and her heart ached with missing him.

"While I was in telepathic contact with the guardian, I felt him escape. Hopefully, he'll be able to find us soon. I could use his help."

"Are the rest of the Angels coming?" Nikki asked.

"They should be here soon if they aren't already settled in the town," Karen said. "Randall's got the rest of the guardians on standby."

Nikki laid a hand on Karen's arm. "Thanks for defending us earlier."

Karen hugged the girl to her. "Well, we've got to stick together, right?"

She nodded. "The younger kids think you're way cool. They want you teach them to kick butt."

Karen patted her shoulder. "Let's get out of this mess first. Where are the others?"

Nikki stepped back. "In the other room. James made all of us stay there so we didn't disturb you. Come on. I'll introduce you."

She led Karen to a small bedroom at the back of the cabin. The children sat on the floor around James as he told them a story. He looked up at her. "Are you okay?"

Karen nodded. "I think it's time to go over this

place inch by inch. Even if we have no way out, we might find something to use to defend ourselves. Spread out, troops. Look everywhere, including the ceiling."

She held James back as the others left the room. "How old are you?"

"Seventeen."

"And the youngest?"

He frowned. "Five. Why?"

She could see questions burning in his face. "Can all of you change at will?"

He shook his head. "No. Just four of us."

She lowered her voice when some of the group came near. "When we get out of here, the younger kids will be defenseless. I'm going to need you older kids to protect them."

James nodded, his eyes serious. "I'll tell them what to do."

She watched his expression darken. "What's wrong?"

He hung his head. "I should've been able to protect them from the start. I shouldn't have needed help. I'm the son of Caledon, strongest leader in the history of the northeast pack. Why couldn't I do anything?"

Karen pulled him close, holding him while his tears soaked her shirt. "It's okay," she murmured as his arms wrapped tightly around her. "Let it out."

They stood like that for a few minutes until Karen felt him pull away. "I'm sorry," he said, wiping his eyes. "I shouldn't have shown weakness."

She cupped his face. "James, you're a teenager. You're allowed a little uncertainty and weakness from time to time."

"You won't tell the others?"

She ruffled his hair. "Your secret's safe with me."

Nikki burst into the room. "We think we found something."

Chapter Seventeen

Nikki pointed to the ceiling at the very end of the hallway. "Matt found it. It looks like a trap door."

Karen narrowed her eyes. The seam was almost invisible unless one concentrated. "You're right. There must be some kind of attic or crawl space." She turned to the pack children. "Can somebody give me a boost?"

James waved to a teen who towered over the group. "Come on, Matt."

Karen steadied herself as the two boys lifted her by her legs. She pushed on the square, feeling a slight resistance. She shoved harder and the panel popped free. Using her elbows, she levered herself up into a cramped, dusty crawl space that ran the length of the cabin. She stood, whacking her head on the low ceiling. "*Ow!*"

"Are you okay?" James called.

She looked down at them and waved. "It's a little tight up here. I'm going to take a look around. Be right back."

The first thing Karen noticed was a small camera at the edge of the trapdoor. She followed the wires to more cameras aimed at the other rooms of the cabin. She wanted to unplug them, but had a feeling that wasn't such a good idea. If they were being monitored right now, someone could be on their way up to the cabin as soon as they saw her right in the lens. She hoped that whoever was watching right now was on a bathroom break or something. She continued checking out the crawl space.

She finally stuck her head through the opening. "There seems to be some sort of small window, but I can't get it open. I think it's locked on the outside." She sat on the edge, dangling her legs through the opening. "It's getting dark up here, so we're going to have to put off any plan until tomorrow. Watch out. I'm coming down."

Karen turned around and felt Matt and James grab her. She slid the panel into place before letting herself be lowered to the floor. She brushed herself off and herded them all back to the bedroom. "They've got cameras up there, and there's no way of knowing if they saw me get into the crawl space."

She stared at them, her breath catching, seeing so many emotions on their faces. Get a grip, she thought. They need you. "I think we can get out of here. Once we leave, we won't be safe anywhere. We can't trust anyone except the wood folk or the guardians, if we can find them."

"Matt and I will stay with the younger kids." James said. "We've got the most fighting experience."

Karen nodded. "Good."

Nikki spoke up. "Owen and I will help you. We don't have any fighting experience, but we've had training."

Karen smiled. Their willingness to help touched her. "Well, you're all about to get some serious OJT." At the younger kids' confused looks, she clarified, "On the job training." She took a deep breath, letting it out slowly. "I've got a confession to make. I don't know where we are or how to contact the guardian."

James laid a hand on her arm. "We'll be all right."

Nikki grinned at the group. "Sure we will. We've got our own Angel to guide us."

Karen gazed at the expectant faces staring at her. I won't let them down, she silently vowed. "Get some rest. Tomorrow, we're out of here."

She crossed to the small window. *I hope I can contact the wood folk. I have a feeling I'm going to need all the help I can get.*

****

Only a little longer until sunset. Randall ducked out the basement entrance, running straight for the wood shed. He darted inside, catching his breath and making sure he wasn't seen. He peeked out, and seeing no one, ran for the woods. He had to contact Raesheen and the rest of the fairy court.

The trees closed around him as he tore through the underbrush. Branches slapped at his face and thorns snagged his clothes. He paused, his breathing heavy, and listened to the sounds around him. He could hear the stream off to his left. Calling Brek would be the quickest way to spread the word through the fairy realm.

Something heavy slammed into him from behind. He flipped over and saw a large badger growling at him as blackbirds gathered in the trees around him. Two dived screaming, aiming for his eyes. He threw his arm over his face, crying out as the birds ripped away hunks of his flesh. He shot to his feet, taking off for what protection the trees would give him. A fox joined the chase, snapping at his legs.

More animals poured from the woods, jumping at

him. He flung squirrels from his back and chest, slapped birds from his hair, and stopped running long enough to kick the fox. "Stop," he commanded. "I don't want to hurt you!" He blocked another attack from the birds, cringing as the burning scratches cut deep into his arm.

Harmon stepped out from the trees. "But they want to hurt you." He walked toward Randall, the animals following him. "They're completely in my power. There's nothing you or any of the fairy folk can do to break the hold I've got over them. Your magic is weak, Dupré. I own them."

Randall didn't move. He glared at Harmon. "I'm betting if I kill you that would work to free them."

Harmon laughed. "It might, but you won't get the chance to find out." He pointed at Randall. "Kill him."

Randall ran again, hearing the animals on his heels. "Damn it," he muttered. He jumped into the stream, slipping and tripping on the loose stones on the bottom. "Brek," he panted. "I could really use your help."

She appeared next to him. "What happened to you?"

He pointed at the menagerie chasing him. "I need a distraction."

Brek turned to the animals, pulling water into herself, towering over the group on the bank. "You have come far enough," she thundered, her voice pounding the air around them. "Return." She swept her arms wide, sending a cascade of water at them, pushing them far back into the woods.

Randall stumbled out on the opposite bank, collapsing on the muddy ground. He sucked air into his lungs, watching as Brek reduced herself to her normal size. "Thanks. They were really doing a number on me."

"It will be sunset soon," she said softly. "You'll be able to heal." She gave him a condescending smile. "I've never seen anyone get hurt as much as you."

He grinned. "My mother says I'm just lucky. My father calls me a trouble magnet." The smile disappeared and he looked away. "I killed someone, Brek."

Brek flowed to sit near him. "Who, Guardian?"

"Edna Strathmore. She had me completely in her control. She wanted..." He stopped. "Let's just say she wanted something I wasn't willing to give. My soul mate sent me her power to help me." He looked at the ground. "I broke Strathmore's neck."

Brek swirled around him. "I know you don't like killing, but again, you've had to take a life out of necessity. It was you or her, my friend, and the realm is always glad when you choose you."

He raised his eyes to the nixie. "But what will my soul mate think?"

Brek placed her fingers under his chin. "You must have faith, guardian. She has not turned from you, even after finding out who you are. Trust that she will understand this. It is your nature and the nature of what you do."

He nodded slowly, then stood, trying to wipe some of the mud from his pants. "I need you to take a message to the wood folk," he said, not looking at her. "Karen and the children are in serious trouble. Troyington has issued orders for their deaths. Get everyone searching."

Brek frowned. "This is dire news. What about the

cabin? Could they be there?"

Randall shook his head, finally looking at her. "They've never been seen there. It's possible Troyington wanted us to get sidetracked by that place so we wouldn't search anywhere else. Ignore the cabin. Go farther up in the hills."

The sky turned a deep blue, fading to purple. Brek watched it for a moment. "The sun's going down. Hurry. The guardian is needed."

"Tell Raesheen to meet me in the clearing."

Brek flowed back into the stream. "Take care, Guardian."

He nodded. "You, too." He ran into the woods, taking his shortcut to the clearing where he and Raesheen always met. He could feel the change starting and stripped off his shirt. He burst into the clearing, yanking off his pants and dropping them on the ground.

The dryad was there, holding out a pair of large shorts. "I didn't think you brought your spare pants." She threw them at him as he finished his nightly transformation. "We can't have you fighting bad guys in naught but what you were graced with at birth."

He pulled up the shorts he had made specifically for his larger form. Raesheen guided his tail through the hole in the back as he finished adjusting them. "I don't know what I'd do without you."

"Let's not find out." She stood back, watching him stretch his wings, his claws digging into the soft earth. "Brek says the situation is more desperate than we knew."

He nodded. "Troyington's finally ordered the pack children to be executed. We've had no luck finding them. The cabin we pinned our hopes on is a bust. With the animals still under Harmon's control, we're out of sources." He stared at the rising moon. "They could be anywhere, and now Karen's with them."

Raesheen hopped on a tree stump. "If your soul mate is with the children, they're in good hands. She won't let anything happen to them." She punched his arm. "And if I know you, you won't let a little thing like no information stop you."

He grinned. "Look higher in the hills. We'll expand the search from there." He grabbed her in a tight hug. "And be careful. I don't want you to get hurt."

She held him a moment longer. "You too."

He propelled himself into the air as Raesheen disappeared into the tree.

Night Angel

Chapter Eighteen

The sun streamed in through the windows, splashing Karen across the face. She stretched, rubbing her eyes as she sat up. There was no Randall this morning to massage the kinks out of her neck. She was cold, inside and out. She touched his power to feel some comfort. She closed her eyes and concentrated, hearing the fairy music again that had become part of her. With Randall's power and the music, she didn't feel so alone. Time to wake the kids.

She went to the back room, watching them sleep for a few minutes. The four older teens held the younger kids, trying to make them comfortable. All of them had dark circles under their eyes, and they looked too thin. She wondered how long it had been since they'd all had a good night's rest and a decent meal. She closed her eyes, wishing she could do more for them.

She clapped her hands, smiling as they groaned. "Wakey, wakey, gang. Rise and shine."

The youngest girl trudged over, yawning and tugging on Karen's sleeve. "I have to go to the bathroom."

Karen gave James a pleading look. "Please tell me there's working plumbing."

He nodded, stretching his arms over his head. "That's just about the only thing they did give us. We were told if we wrecked the bathroom, they wouldn't fix it. That stopped any plans we had for bashing them on their heads with heavy porcelain."

She winked. "Good idea." She turned to the others. "Everybody, make sure you take care of business before we go."

The little girl tugged on her sleeve again. "You, too."

Karen knelt next to her. "How about if I go first? Would that make you feel better?"

The girl nodded, then leaned in to whisper loudly, "I guess even Angels have business, right?"

Karen chuckled. "Right."

When she came out, she headed for Nikki. "Is there anything to eat?"

"No." She glanced toward the front door. "We've got plastic cups for water, but no food. Someone usually brings us stuff."

Karen stared at the front door too. "When do they come?"

Nikki shrugged. "Whenever they feel like it. We only get fed once a day."

Great, Karen thought. They could come any time. "James, come with me to the crawl space. We've got to get out of here as soon as possible, and I'm going to need your help."

Matt and Owen lifted them. Karen crawled on her hands and knees, leading James to the small window she'd found the day before. "I'm sure this goes out."

James nodded. "If it didn't before, it's about to."

Karen squeezed over as far as she could. "It's not going to budge by pushing, so we're going to try kicking it."

They lay on their backs, kicking hard at the small door that barred them from the outside. It still wouldn't move an inch.

"Let me half shift. I'll have more leg strength, and we should be able to kick it loose," James said.

She nodded. "Good idea. It'll be a little tight, but it should work."

As James changed halfway to his wolf form, she tapped into the power she shared with Randall. It filled her, making her feel invincible.

James looked at her. "Ready?" he asked, his voice just above a growl.

She grinned at the teen. "Let's do this and get the heck out of here."

She counted to three, and they kicked out as hard as they could. Wood splintered, and they did it again. The third time, the door broke free, falling to the ground below. They crawled forward and peered over the edge. James shifted back to human.

Karen eyed the distance. "It can't be more than fifteen or twenty feet."

James looked at the ground, then back to Karen. "Are you sure? It looks longer than that to me."

She laid a hand on his shoulder. "I'm sure, but I'm going to need your help."

"Name it."

She swung her legs over the edge. "I need you to lower me as far as you can. I'll drop the rest of the way."

James' eyes widened. "What if you get hurt?" he argued. "What if they catch you? What if..."

She patted his shoulder. "It'll be all right. Ready?" He gave her a curt nod. "Then let's do it."

James held her hands and lay on his stomach, pushing himself forward with his feet. She smiled at him as he started lowering her, his arms shaking with the effort. He grit his teeth and moved forward another couple of inches.

"That's it," he gasped. "I can't go any further. I'm too close to the edge."

Karen spared a quick glance down, not as close as she hoped to be. "Okay, let me go." She called on her power as James opened his hands as she fell to the ground.

She relaxed as she hit, bending her legs to absorb the impact and roll out of the fall. She jumped to her feet, hugging the building while she checked the area. No one and no animal was in sight.

She waved to James, who was peering anxiously at her from the window. "I'm okay. Stay there and tell one of the others to meet me at the front door." She watched him disappear then headed around to the front.

The door was as solid as the rest of the cabin. It was banded with the now recognizable dull metal of cold iron and a shinier metal that had to be silver. She shook her head. Troyington really had thought of everything. She touched the silver and felt nothing from it, but the cold iron sent sharp shockwaves zinging through her. The door was sealed with a thick padlock.

She grimaced as she tugged on the lock. It was as solid as the rest. "I will not lose my temper," she growled. She spied a large rock and considered bashing the lock, but hesitated. If Cray and Harmon or whoever was in charge of surveillance saw damage to the lock, they'd know immediately something was up, and she and the children would lose precious time being undiscovered.

"Is anybody there?" she called.

"It's Matt," came the muffled reply.

"There's no way I can open this lock, and the door is banded with silver and cold iron," she called. "I'm going back to the attic window. We're going to have to take everyone out that way. Tell James and start getting everyone up in the crawl space."

Karen hurried to the back of the cabin. "James, I want you to start lowering the kids down. I'll catch them." Karen glanced around, expecting to see Troyington and his men coming any second. Their luck had to run out soon.

Matt held James by the ankles so he could hang further out. As Karen caught the pack children, she made them stand next to the cabin so, hopefully, they would be harder to spot.

"There's only Matt and me left," James called. "I'm coming next."

Matt held him by his wrists, lowering him as far as possible and Karen and Owen grabbed him as he fell.

He waved to Matt. "Come on."

Matt waved everyone away. "Stand back. I'm too big for you guys to catch."

Karen looked up at the large boy. "Matt, make sure you stay loose. Bend your legs, and that will help when you hit."

He nodded and squeezed out the small window. He hung by his hands for a second then let go, hitting the ground with a solid thump. He kept his legs bent and when he hit the ground, he stumbled backwards a few steps before ending up on his butt.

Karen walked over to him, extending her hand.

"Are you okay?"

He took her hand, blushing as she pulled him to his feet. "Yeah. I never said I was graceful."

She brushed him off. "Grace will come in time." She looked at the kids watching her. "Let's get out of here."

She led them around to the front. "This is probably the more dangerous way, but it's the most sensible." She pointed to the trees. "See that path there? It's sloping downward, which is the way we need to go." She turned to them. "As soon as any animal sees us we'll be on the run. I'm going to need you older kids to help the younger ones keep up."

James stepped forward. "Do you think we'll be able to contact the wood folk soon?"

Karen sighed. "I hope so." She eyed the open distance to the trees. "We've got to go. Is everyone ready?" They murmured they were, but Karen heard uncertainty in their voices. "James, Matt, you guys bring up the rear. Nikki, Owen, stay near me."

The group moved away from the safety of the building, running for the safety of the woods. Karen blew out a sigh of relief as the trees surrounded them, not feeling nearly as exposed as she did in the open ground. She held her hand up as voices drifted to her. She motioned them to get off the path and hide themselves in the thick underbrush.

"Mr. Troyington said I can twist her head off her skinny neck," Cray said, malicious glee coloring his words.

"It's going to be hard work, killing them all," Harmon cautioned.

"Nothing we can't handle."

Karen shivered, and not from the chill in the early morning air. The men's words sliced through her, stabbing at her heart. Time was officially up. "We've got to run," she whispered to Nikki.

The girl nodded and passed the word down the line. "We're ready."

Karen crouched, taking off in a slow run, wanting to hurry, but keeping her young charges in mind. The gurgling of a stream reached her and she veered off toward it as the angry screaming of birds reached her. Risking a glance behind, she saw them massing in a black cloud, heading right for them.

"James," Karen called. "You and Matt take the others and head for the stream. Call the water nixies. Nikki, Owen, and I will try and hold off the animals."

James squeezed her arm. "Be safe." He pushed through the brush, Matt herding the children along behind.

Karen checked to see where Nikki and Owen stood. They were off to her left and right, a few steps behind. "We'll try not to hurt them," Karen said. "The animals are still under Harmon's control. It's not their fault what they're being made to do."

"We know," Owen said. "But the pack comes first."

Karen gave him a small smile. The sandy-haired teen seemed like the serious one of the pack children. She wouldn't fault him at all if he used extreme force. She nodded at him. "I understand. Let's try, though, to keep the casualties to a minimum."

"We'll try," Nikki said. She pointed over Karen's shoulder. "Here they come."

Karen dropped back to her defensive posture as she

felt more than saw the werewolves shift. She threw her arms up, protecting her face as the blackbirds dove at them in a solid wave.

"Ow, damn it!" She yanked a bird none too gently from her hair, feeling like half her scalp went with it. Wave after wave of birds hit them, the tide seeming to never end. She grit her teeth as her arms started to feel like lead. Where are they all coming from? she thought.

She heard the growls and snarls from the werewolves and knew they were holding their own. *Don't look at the kids. They're fine.* She blocked two more birds as they dove at her head, their ceaseless calling grating on her nerves.

A last squawk and the attack was over. Bodies of birds littered the ground at their feet. The teens shifted back to human, their clothes tattered but mostly intact. The three of them were covered with scratches and blood smears.

Karen dabbed at the blood running from her scalp. "Stupid bird," she mumbled.

Owen approached her slowly. "Angel, are you okay?"

She took a deep breath, letting it out slowly. "As well as can be expected." She looked at the carnage at their feet again. "That wasn't so hard."

The three looked at each other, then burst out laughing. Karen draped her arms around their shoulders. "Come on. Let's catch up to the others."

Chapter Nineteen

They ran toward the stream and burst into a small clearing to see James and Matt fighting off an army of animals trying to get to the others. The three leapt in, Karen landing a solid kick on a large badger. Owen threw a fox into the trees as Nikki scooped an armload of squirrels to toss them as far as she could.

The attack slowed, then stopped as the animals backed away, finally running off into the woods. James half shifted, growling at two foxes who appeared to need a little more incentive to join their fellows.

"Everyone okay?" Karen asked, looking around at the children.

James shifted back, eyeing the three of them. "Looks like we fared better than you guys. What happened?"

Karen shook her head. "Birds. Lots of them."

They all turned to her. "So, what's next?" Matt asked.

She wanted to tell them it would be simple now, but it would be a lie. "Believe it or not, that was the easy part. They know we're free and the general direction we're heading. Unless we can get in touch with the wood folk, we're on our own."

James stood in front of the pack. "If you want to try to contact a water nixie, we'll stand guard. Nixies are the fastest way to get news through the fairy realm.

Whoever lives in this part of the stream may know a faster way back to the guardian."

She clapped him on the shoulder. "Good thinking." She pulled the smaller children to her. "You guys stay with me and watch my back while the others protect us." They nodded and she smiled at the fierce determination on their young faces.

Karen sat on the damp ground and trailed shaking fingers in the stream. She had no idea what she was doing and was only imitating what she had seen Randall do. Soon, she could feel the power inside her glow brighter as it leaked from her fingers into the water swirling around her hand. "If there's anyone here, I need your help."

The water bubbled and swirled, forming into a large man. He scowled at her, pulling water into himself, giving him a terrifying appearance. "How have you learned to summon a nixie?"

Karen rose to her feet, not afraid, only relieved at finding help. "I'm so sorry to bother you, but these children and I desperately need your help."

The youngest girl ran forward, her face shining with joy. "Lael, you're here!"

The nixie reduced his size to peer at her. "Ari?" He stared at Karen. "You've rescued Caledon's pack children?"

Karen watched him rise to look her in the eye. "Sort of. I need to get in touch with Raesheen, and I really need to find the guardian."

He flowed around her as Brek had done, gazing at her from all sides before once again looking into her eyes. "You and the guardian are soul mates. The bond between you is stronger than any I've ever felt."

She reached out her hand as she stepped closer to him. "Cray and Harmon are after us. We need to get out of this area as soon as possible."

He flowed back into the stream. "I can lead you as far as the stream allows. As we travel, I will send a message to the wood folk and let them know where to meet you."

"Thank you so much." Karen ran to get the others. "Let's go. Lael's going to take us as far as he can. We should have help waiting for us a little farther down the hill."

The group ran beside the stream as Lael flowed beside them. At times, he vanished, and they heard splashing and yelps from animals. Karen grinned. The nixie was certainly taking no prisoners.

As the trees thinned, Lael stopped them. "The stream bends in a different direction than you need to go. I've gotten in touch with members of the fairy court. Wait here. Someone should come soon."

Karen bowed deeply to the water nixie. "Thank you so much for all your help. If there's ever anything I can do for you, please don't hesitate to call on me."

He smiled at her. "I will remember your kind offer." He disappeared, becoming part of the stream that was his home.

"Okay, gang, take five." She waved them all to the ground and gestured to James. "I want you guys to stand watch. I'm going to check the woods around us."

James nodded. "All right, Angel." He waved Owen over. "You've got the best sense of smell. Shift and give a yell if anyone but the Angel comes near."

"Will do." Owen stripped out of his clothes, then shifted, keeping his nose pointed to the air.

Karen walked into the surrounding brush, careful not to go too far. She turned to look at the small pack. James was getting everyone settled and scanning the area around them. The teen was shaping up to be a good leader.

"Miss!" a tiny voice cried.

Karen smiled as Dayla hit her square in the face. She was never so glad to see someone in her life. "I missed you, Dayla."

The fairy backed up, hovering about six inches away from Karen's nose. "When Troyington took you, I couldn't get to you. The metal stopped me. Then you disappeared and I couldn't find you." Dayla brightened. "But I heard you yesterday when you told me to help the guardian. I tried, miss, but I couldn't get to him."

"I knew you'd hear me." Karen frowned. "Has anyone seen the guardian since yesterday?"

Dayla nodded eagerly. "Yes, miss. He joined with Raesheen last night and is actively looking for all of you."

Karen sagged with relief. He was safe. She closed her eyes, feeling his arms around her and seeing his impish grin that made her melt.

"So, you ready to help me save these kids?" she asked Dayla, her mouth curling up in a wide smile.

Dayla snapped off a salute. "Yes, miss. Raesheen has sent most of the court to guard us as I take you back to the guardian. They'll be hidden, but watching."

The two headed back to the kids and James ran over to them. "Owen's detected someone coming."

Karen glanced over her shoulder at the trees. Knowing the wood folk were there made the knot in her stomach finally start to relax. But someone was out there who wanted to do them harm. Time to get moving. "Let's go. We've only got a couple of hours of daylight left. Dayla, where can we stay tonight that's sheltered?"

The fairy motioned for them to follow her and she flew ahead. "I'll show you."

"James, take the lead," Karen said, not being able to stop looking for whoever was coming. "I'll bring up the rear."

They set off at a quick pace. Karen felt the ground slope more and more under her feet as she hiked. She glanced over her shoulder again, still not seeing anyone. The girl, Ari, tripped and fell, skinning her knee.

Karen helped her up. "Are you okay?"

Ari sniffed hard as tears rolled down her face, her bottom lip trembling. "I'm tired and hungry, and I want to go home."

Karen smoothed her hair back. "I know, sweetie," she murmured. "We're headed that way now." She pulled the girl close, holding her as she cried. She looked up as James approached.

"Is she okay?" he asked.

Karen nodded. "She's just a little tired. She fell and hurt her knee."

Ari turned and held her leg up. "See?"

James tried not to smile. "Come on, Ari. I'll carry you for a while. Then at least you won't be tired." James knelt down, letting her climb onto his back. He jogged back to the front of the line. "Let's move, people."

The sky turned lavender as the sun began to set. Dayla stopped them at the edge of the woods and pointed to a small cabin. "We can stay here tonight. No one's been here in months."

Karen wondered if that was the decoy cabin and turned to the children. "Stay here. James, come with me."

They slowly crept up to the front door. Karen turned the knob and the door swung in, raising the hairs on the back of her neck. "I don't like this," she muttered.

"Me neither," James said in a low voice. "But we need to check it out. It's going to get cold tonight, and the little kids can't stay out in it."

Karen nodded. "Let's do it."

This had to be the cabin the wood folk had pinned their hopes on. The two of them entered side by side, scanning the room. The smell of new wood, paint, and varnish hit them as soon as they opened the door. Karen saw the furniture wrapped in plastic and knew this was the hunters' cabin Bradford rented out. They split up, Karen heading for the kitchen, and James, checking out the bedroom and small bathroom. They met back in the living room.

"There's no food, but there's running water," Karen said. She flipped a switch on the wall. "And no power."

"There's plenty of blankets in a closet in the bedroom," James said. "This place stinks of a trap."

"I agree." Karen stared at the living room, nodding toward the fireplace. "But the kids are tired, and we need to be out of the cold. I think we'll risk a fire so we can keep warm."

James chuckled. "It's not like they don't know which way we're going anyway."

"Exactly. You get a fire going. I'll get the kids."

Karen trotted to where the group waited.

She took a deep breath. "This place looks okay, but James is worried it might be a set-up. I need you guys to do what we say in case there's trouble."

They all nodded, and she led them to the cabin. Karen went in last, locking the door behind her. "Matt and Owen, make sure all the doors and windows are locked. Nikki, go grab some blankets from the back room. I'm going to see about getting some water for us."

She handed out the small cups and watched as they drank it all. They slowly settled down as the blankets and the fire warmed them. Karen went over to James. "Get some rest. I'll take the first watch."

He nodded and chose a spot near Nikki. Karen smiled as the girl readjusted herself, laying her head on James' shoulder. Definitely a relationship in the making. Her thoughts turned to Randall. What she wouldn't give to be curled up with him like that right now. Closing her eyes, she pictured him holding her as he smiled. Loneliness crawled through her, making her want to run down the hillside and find him. She wanted to feel those rough fingers caress her. She wanted his arms around her. She wanted to lose herself in those magical wild eyes.

Karen, can you hear me?

Karen stopped as the telepathic contact touched her. *Rena? Thank heavens.*

Where're you at? We can't get any information from anyone in this lousy town.

Karen could hear Rena's annoyance. *I'm not sure. I'm in a cabin in the woods somewhere. Keep an eye on the people there. You'll know when things start going down.*

We'll keep our eyes open.

Karen smiled, even though she knew Rena couldn't see it. *Thanks, Red.*

****

James shook her the next morning as sunlight sparkled throughout the cabin. "Wake up, Angel. Someone's coming."

Dayla took to the air as Karen jumped to her feet, staring at the door. "Is it Troyington?"

James shook his head. "We don't know. We can't get a good look."

She laid her hand on his shoulder. "Stay inside. Keep everyone away from the windows. Check out back just in case whoever it is isn't alone. And lock the front door when I leave."

James nodded as Matt took off for the back of the cabin. He opened the door just wide enough for her to squeeze out, then pushed it shut, clicking the lock.

Karen, people are starting to leave town. They could be coming your way, Rena said telepathically.

Understood. Do what you can on that end. I'll take care of things here. Karen stepped off the porch while she was in contact with Rena. She turned to the fairy hovering by her head. "Dayla, get the wood folk. This is it."

The tiny fairy took off as Karen ducked behind a large tree, watching the intruder's shadow approach.

Close enough, she thought. She sprung out, struck his chest, then knocked him to the ground with a leg sweep. "Wrong cabin, buddy."

Randall groaned from the ground and rubbed his chest. "Remind me never to startle you."

Karen's hands flew to her mouth. Randall was here! He was safe! She threw herself on top of him, straddling his lap. Grabbing his shirt, she kissed him fiercely.

"Where have you been?" she demanded. "I was scared something had happened to you." She kissed him again, feeling him respond favorably to her greeting.

He grinned, holding her by her waist, running his thumbs over her ribs. "I went to call the guardians. They're in the town. They've told Caledon the children are free."

She pushed his hair off his face. "We need to go inside before the children get an impromptu demonstration of Sex Ed."

He winked at her as his hands moved slowly upward to brush against her breast. They barely got in the door when Randall was mobbed by the werewolf children.

James came away from the window, clasping Randall's hand before allowing himself to be pulled into a tight hug. James stood back, his face serious.

"Troyington's coming," the teen said. "And he's not alone."

Chapter Twenty

Troyington, Cray, and Harmon strode across the front yard with about twenty men from the town, splitting off to circle the building. The sheriff marched behind Troyington toward the cabin.

"Come out with your hands up, Dupré," Troyington called. "The sheriff is here to arrest you for the murder of Edna Strathmore."

Karen turned to Randall and he nodded, confirming the accusation. "I didn't have a choice."

Karen squeezed his hand. "I understand. When you told me what was happening, if I had been there, I would've killed her myself."

Randall gave her a quick smile before turning to stare out the window. "I'm going out there."

"Are you crazy?" Karen asked. "They're going to kill you."

James walked over. "The Angel is right, Guardian. You can't go without us."

Randall smiled at James, then turned to Karen, laying a hand on her cheek. "I wasn't planning on being alone for long. When they approach, you, James, and Matt come out. Nikki, you and Owen stay in here with the kids."

Matt slammed his fist into his open palm. "Is it finally butt-kicking time?"

Randall gave him a thumbs up. "Yes. Today, all

this ends." He pulled Karen close to him, kissing her hard. "Let's have the end to our story."

"Please be careful," she whispered.

He grinned. "I'm always careful."

Karen elbowed him lightly in the ribs. "Sure you are."

"Come out, Dupré," Troyington called again. "This is your last chance for this to end peacefully."

Randall stepped out on the porch, his hands at his sides. He strolled over to Troyington and the men around him. "It's over." Randall nodded to the group behind him. "Take your men and leave. The children are with me, and they're safe. I'm no longer bound by the contract I signed."

Troyington stepped closer to him. "Look around you. As always, I've got the superior position. My men outnumber you."

Randall smiled, glancing at the woods surrounding them. "Maybe."

Troyington shoved him. "There's no maybe about it. Give me the brats, and you and your soul mate can leave. Isn't that what you want?"

"What I want," Randall said, "is to see you pay for the crimes you've committed against the northeast pack. Let us take them home before you get hurt."

Troyington picked at invisible lint on his jacket. "I've got many scientists that would be interested in werewolves and gargoyle hybrids. You and the pack aren't leaving here except in cages to go to labs across the country."

"I'm sorry you feel that way," Randall said, glancing over his shoulder as Karen, Matt, and James came out to stand behind him. "But you've chosen how this is going to end. I almost pity you. You have no chance and no clue."

Cray hefted the cold iron bar in his hands. "Now can I kill him?" Troyington waved him ahead. Cray pointed the bar at Randall. "You're dead, southern boy."

He charged Randall, raising the bar high over his head before bringing it down quickly. Randall dodged away from the blow, slamming his fist into Cray's stomach, dropping him like a stone. "And you're stupid."

Cray grabbed Randall's ankle, pulling his leg out from under him. As Randall hit the ground, Cray brought his fist down hard on his chest. Cray's face twisted into an evil sneer as Randall gasped for breath. The two struggled to their feet and separated, eyeing each other.

****

Karen watched as Randall faced off with the bigger man. Suddenly, she saw something black move out of the corner of her eye. Before she knew it, blackbirds swarmed over them, diving at her and the two teens.

"Guys!" Karen cried. *"Look out!"*

Karen pointed to Harmon standing near the trees. "Harmon's in the back. We've got to stop him!" She saw the wood folk emerge, heading straight for the men circling the cabin. She felt the familiar nudge of telepathic contact.

Karen, Rena called through the telepathic link. *Mist, Metamorph, and I have stopped a lot more of the people here from leaving town. Do you need help where you are?*

Not yet. Just keep things under control there. I've

got help here.

"Harmon's mine," James said, then fully shifted, his eyes never leaving the stable master for a second as his lips drew back over long teeth, and he growled deep in his chest. He sprang forward, heading straight for the stable master. Animals tried to stop him as he bowled over the larger ones, ignored the smaller ones, and leapt on his target in a fury of brown and silver fur.

Karen glimpsed Troyington move in behind her and swing at her head. She pivoted, throwing her arms up, blocking his punch. Sweeping his arm aside, she countered with an open palm strike to his chest, staggering him back.

She shook her head. "Hitting from behind isn't nice." She swung her leg around in a roundhouse kick, silently swearing when he dodged it. His arm came around for a strike she barely had time to block.

He grabbed her arm, twisting it behind her and leaned close to her ear. "All this resistance for nothing. If we win, you'll be dead. If you win, my men will burn the cabin with the wolves inside."

She turned to him, her face inches from his. "Bradford, there's something I've been wanting to tell you for a long time now."

He smiled at her, making her skin crawl. "Oh? And what would that be?"

She stomped on his instep, then rammed her elbow back into his solar plexus. As he fell to the ground, she stood over him. *"Stop touching me!"*

A yelp of pain to her right drew her attention from Troyington. James, bleeding heavily from a knife wound on his shoulder, had Harmon on the ground. Karen started over to him, but Troyington grabbed her leg, yanking her to the ground as he drew a slim dagger.

"I brought this to deal with Dupré," he panted. "It'll do the job on you too." He swung it in a wide arc, grazing Karen's arm. She cried out and he smiled, a maniacal gleam in his eyes as he brought the blade down. "It causes you the same pain as Dupré? Good."

Karen grabbed her arm, the pain from the blade excruciating, making her eyes water. If it hurt her this badly, what did Randall feel from it?

****

Cray twirled the bar in his hands, giving Randall a condescending look. "I guess this is it."

Randall nodded. "I told you before, there's not going to be enough of you left for people to mourn over. I mean to keep that particular promise."

Cray laughed. "Still talking the big talk. Come on, then. Let's see if you can do it." He swung the bar at Randall's head.

Randall threw his arm up, crying out when the cold iron seared his flesh, breaking the bone. He held his arm close to his chest, ducking under Cray's next swing, then kicked him in the crotch, smiling as the big man grabbed himself and fell to his knees.

Cray glared at him as he climbed to his feet, and swung the bar again, this time connecting with Randall's side. Randall cried out again, feeling flesh burn and ribs break. He hadn't thought Cray would fight this long or this hard. The man was a *coward*. Where had the steel in his spine come from? Cray jabbed him hard in the chest, and Randall felt his skin bubble through his shirt.

Randall slammed his head into Cray's face, breaking the bigger man's nose. He kicked out, catching Cray in the knee. Cray rained down blows with the cold iron bar, driving Randall to his knees. The pain seared through his skin, feeling like it was burning his soul.

Randall gritted his teeth as he yanked the metal bar from Cray's hands, feeling his skin bubble and seeing smoke rise from his palm as the metal burned him. Blood dripped from his hand as his eyes watered and he clamped his teeth together to stop the scream building in his throat. He slammed it down on the big man's skull again and again until Cray quit moving. Throwing the bar down, he drew a ragged breath as he looked at the damage he'd done to himself. Randall heard a moan from the ground and turned as a blur of black and gray fur streaked by him.

Randall watched the werewolf make short work of the big man and smiled. "Good job, Matt."

A sparkle of sunlight to his right caught his attention. He turned, seeing Troyington stab at Karen. "No!" He ran toward them.

Randall saw Troyington's head snap up, and the rich man's eyes widened. In that split-second, Randall tackled him, taking both of them to the ground. Randall rolled out of it, rising to one knee and cradling his arm while Troyington climbed to his feet.

"Damn you!" Troyington screamed, driving the cold iron blade into and down Randall's chest, ripping open his flesh in a jagged cut. Randall fell to his knees before crumpling to the ground as Troyington ran for the trees.

"No!" Karen shouted. She dropped to the ground next to him, laying his head in her lap. "Someone, anyone, over here!"

Raesheen appeared next to her. "Great Mother Earth, not him."

Karen grabbed Raesheen's sleeve. "He was stabbed with a cold iron blade. Do something!" she begged. "Help him!"

Raesheen waved Matt and James over. "Take him inside. Be gentle now."

They carried Randall to the small bedroom. Raesheen ripped his shirt open so she could see the wound. The edges of the knife wound had already begun to blacken as the rest of his skin blistered. She shook her head. He must have taken a lot of damage in the fight with Cray for the black to spread so quickly.

"He's got cold iron poisoning." Raesheen looked up at Karen. "I need help. Stay with him. I'll return soon." The dryad ran from the room.

Karen took Randall's hand, kissing his knuckles. "You can't leave me," she choked out. "You promised me you wouldn't be dumb enough to get yourself killed."

Raesheen returned a few minutes later, followed by a gnome with leathery brown skin and white hair that stood out in every direction from his head. The dryad laid a pile of herbs on the table next to the bed. She gestured to the gnome. "This is Gizel. He's the best healer in the realm."

Karen stared at him. "What can I do?"

Gizel stared at her, narrowing his eyes. "You and the guardian are soul mates?" She nodded. "And you've shared power?"

She nodded again. "Yes. I can feel his power in me. It's so dim. I'm afraid."

"No," Gizel barked. "No fear. When I tell you, call

the power forth and pour it into him. You understand?"

Karen nodded, opening her mouth to say something, but no words came out.

"Good." The gnome turned to Raesheen. "The salve must be very strong this time. Stronger than any you've made before."

Raesheen bowed to Gizel. "Give me a couple of minutes."

Karen watched Gizel as he examined her soul mate. He muttered to himself as he checked the severity of Randall's injuries. The black around the wound was spreading, making him check frequently for the dryad.

Raesheen finally entered, carrying a large bowl with both hands. The rising steam filled the room with a pungent, yet sweet, scent. She stood next to Gizel, who spooned a large glob of the concoction onto Randall's chest. He smoothed it into the wound while muttering an incantation, making the salve glow pale pink. He took what was left, spooned some onto Randall's hand, and repeated the incantation.

He sat back and looked at Karen. "Call the power. Keep him with you no matter what. I'll be back before sunset." The gnome turned on his heel, waddling from the room.

Karen pulled up the power in her, touching his mind as she did. She poured the power into him like she had before. "You'd better be in there," she told him.

He was, but silent.

Pain filtered into her mind from him. She welcomed it. If he was feeling pain, then he was alive. She pulled more of it into her, trying to take it all from him. She could see her silver dragon fold around his pale purple gargoyle, cradling it in its coils.

She stroked his hair, placing a small kiss on his forehead. "You can't leave me now that we've won. You promised."

****

Karen sat up when the door creaked open. Gizel entered, heading straight for Randall. He checked the salve on the knife wound, nodding in satisfaction.

He gazed at Karen. "He'll live, but he'll have a scar."

Karen sagged back in the chair. *He's going to live.* "I don't care if he scars." She dropped to her knees, grabbing Gizel in a tight hug. "Thank you so much."

He patted her back. "The bond between the two of you is one of the strongest I've ever felt. Keep it going through the night. He should wake tomorrow. Stay with him. Watch over him."

She gazed at Randall in the bed. "I will. I promise."

Gizel noticed blood on her sleeve and lifted it, muttering something. He took some of the salve and smeared it on her and said the incantation one last time. He nodded and left.

The setting sun bathed the room in low light. Raesheen came in. "Gizel says he's going to pull through."

Karen nodded, glancing out the window at the darkening sky. "Will he change?"

Raesheen walked to the bed, nodding as she threw back the covers. "If we got the poison out of his system in time. Help me get him undressed."

They pulled his clothes off as the last rays of the sun faded. When Karen had lit the last candle Raesheen had brought, the guardian lay there. "Will the change help him heal?"

Raesheen shrugged. "It should. Take a quick break. I'll stay with him."

Karen stood and stretched. She watched Randall a few more minutes before forcing herself to leave the room.

She went to the kitchen for some water. As she filled the glass, she saw movement outside. She eased herself out the door, staying close to the cabin wall. As her eyes became accustomed to the darkness, she saw several men, but they looked larger than normal and deformed.

"Who are you and what are you doing here?" she demanded.

The largest stepped forward. "We mean you no harm. We're guardians. One of our own is here and injured. We were fighting the men in the woods when he was hurt."

"Guardians?" Karen repeated. She ran to him, throwing her arms around his waist. No wonder they looked odd. Now she could make out their wings and tails and their elongated faces. "I'm so glad you're here. I'm Karen."

The guardian looked down at her. "You're the one the children call Angel?"

"Yes." Karen stepped back and smiled.

One of the guardians came forward. His ebony hair fell over his eyes as he stared at her. "Is Randall all right?"

Karen nodded, narrowing her eyes. He had the same deep, southern drawl as Randall. "Gizel seems to think so, and he changed at sunset. I'm hoping he'll heal faster."

He grabbed her hands. "That's great news. If the

wound had been any more life threatening, he wouldn't have changed." He stared at the cabin. "Can I see him?"

"Who are you?" she whispered.

"My name's Marshall. I'm his brother."

Chapter Twenty-One

Karen's eyes fluttered open and she stretched, arching her back to work the kinks out. She smiled when she saw Randall watching her.

He held out his hand and she hurried to his side. "Morning, beautiful."

She sat on the bed, taking his hand in hers. "Morning, yourself. Gizel said if your wound looks better you can keep the bandage off."

"I'm all yours."

He lay still while she checked his chest. "All closed up. I think you should keep it covered for at least one more day." She took clean gauze from the night stand.

"I can't believe it's over," he said, watching her work.

She smiled at him. "How's your arm?"

He flexed it. "Still aches, but the bones have mended."

She took the bandage off his hand, nodding in satisfaction when his skin was pink and healthy, not the angry red mass of blood and blisters that had covered his palm the day before. "And your ribs?"

He nodded. "The same as the rest of me."

"That good, huh?" She dropped her gaze to his bare chest with the stark white bandage. "Gizel says you're going to scar."

He curled his fingers around her hand. "Badge of honor. It was worth it to save you."

She leaned over, stroking his hair. "The guardians came to the cabin last night. One in particular wants to see you. His name is Marshall."

Randall tried to sit up, grimaced, and rubbed his chest. "Marshall's here? He promised me he'd stay away." He glanced up at her. "Marshall's my brother."

"I know," she said, grinning. "I met him last night. He's very worried about you." She went to the door and turned to him. "I'll go get him." She stabbed her finger at him. "And you, stop moving."

She opened the back door, stepping into the bright morning sun. The guardians patrolled close to the cabin, their eyes watching the surrounding area for threats.

She waved to them. "Good morning." *Are all guardians this extraordinarily handsome?* she thought. As humans, the ease and grace with which they moved and their extreme good looks could make a sinner out of a saint. Misty would have a lot of candidates for her list. She couldn't help but smile at the thought.

Marshall trotted over to her. His eyes were stormy gray, perfect with his midnight hair. *He must've broken a lot of hearts in high school.*

"Good morning, Angel." He kissed her cheek. "Can I see him?"

Karen smiled. "He seems a little upset with you. Go on in. He's in the bedroom." She watched as Marshall hurried through the door and down the hallway. She turned to the others. "It's not over, is it?"

"Liam," he said, introducing himself. "And no, it isn't. As long as Troyington lives, the threat remains. Caledon wants the children home as soon as possible.

Marshall and I are going to stay with you and Randall. The rest will escort the children home as soon as they are ready to go."

She nodded. "That sounds great. The children need to be home with their families and to get a decent meal."

He laid his hand on her shoulder. "You and Randall have done enough. We can finish it if he wants."

Karen stared into Liam's eyes. "He'll insist on taking down Troyington. As he's the one that's suffered the most, it's his right."

"I hoped that would be your answer." Liam nodded toward the cabin. "I know where you'd rather be. Go on. We'll talk more later."

"Thank you," she said. "The rest of you will come see him, won't you?"

He gave her a slight smile. "Of course. Just because we're from different clans doesn't mean we aren't tied together. All guardians are bound by who we are and what we do. We're brothers in the truest sense of the word." He gave her a little push toward the cabin. "Now go. He needs you."

As Karen made her way to the bedroom, laughter drifted toward her. She stood in the doorway, watching the brothers. She could see the resemblance now that they were human. Even though Marshall was bigger, with broader shoulders, longer legs, and more muscular arms, they had similar shaped faces and the same impish smiles.

"You guys catching up?" she asked coming into the room.

Randall smiled at her. "Yeah." He turned to

Marshall. "See what I mean?"

Marshall's eyes narrowed as he watched her walk closer to the bed. "Yeah. You've got a seriously powerful soul mate. The High Mother is going to love her. She complements your power perfectly."

"I know."

Karen folded her arms, staring at the two of them. "But he's got this annoying habit of talking about me like I'm not here." The brothers were seriously sexy. Thank goodness Marshall's smile didn't affect her like Randall's. There were many benefits to having one love, after all.

Marshall laughed. "He does it to the rest of us, too. Maybe you'll get him to break that particular habit. Welcome to the family."

"Thanks." Karen was run into from behind as the werewolf children crowded into the room, the younger ones arguing over who got to sit on the bed.

Karen, you awake? Rena called in her mind.

Yeah. What's up?

All the people that left the town yesterday are back, and we've been told in no uncertain terms to leave.

Get out of there then. I'll see you back at Angel Haven in a couple of days.

You sure?

Karen watched the children and Randall laugh and talk. *I'm sure. There are a few loose ends here that need to be tied up. I'll be home soon.*

Finally, Karen clapped her hands to get their attention. "All right, gang," she said. "The guardians are here to take you home, and Randall needs some more rest. We'll join you tomorrow."

The pack children filed out, calling their goodbyes

to Randall and Karen. Marshall stood, too. "I'll let you guys have some time. I'll be back later, little brother."

She shut the door behind Marshall and went to take the hand Randall held out to her. She shrieked as he pulled her down onto the bed with him.

"You're going to aggravate your injury," she said.

"Tough," he murmured, kissing her lightly. He trailed his fingers along her arm as he inhaled her scent. "When I saw the knife, I was so afraid I'd lose you. I just want to hold you, to know you're safe."

She snuggled closer, sighing as his arms wrapped around her. "I'm glad I made you keep your promise."

He raised an eyebrow. "Oh? What promise?"

She traced his jaw. "You promised me you wouldn't be dumb enough to get yourself killed."

He grinned, his hand dropping to her shirt and opening the top button. "Want to help me heal faster?"

Gazing in his eyes, she knew exactly what he meant. "How? Do you need some soup or something?"

He opened another button. "I was thinking more along the lines of a little tender loving care." He opened her shirt the rest of the way, placing light kisses on her collar bone.

She stood, slowly peeling off her clothes. She felt her body burn from the intense hunger in his eyes. "I think soup would be better for you."

He smiled, pulling his power forth. "No, I think you're just what the doctor ordered."

She threw the covers off, and pulling her own power out, straddled his lap. She leaned down and whispered, "Let's make you better."

****

Karen stood and dressed. "The sun's setting soon.

The other guardians want to see you."

Randall carefully sat up, wincing as he felt the knife wound twinge. "Are you coming with me?"

Karen turned to him, running her hand down his arm. "Of course. I'm your soul mate. It's my duty to be with you no matter what."

He winked at her. "I can't wait for this to be over."

"I know. Get yourself ready. I'll see you outside in a few minutes." She pointed to the chair against the far wall. "Raesheen brought your pants." He nodded and Karen slipped out, closing the door behind her.

As the sun began to set, Randall climbed from the bed. His nightly change was beginning, and he welcomed it. He could feel himself grow stronger as his body morphed into the gargoyle. Folding his wings tightly around him, he trod carefully through the cabin to join his brethren.

He stepped outside, unfurling his wings to their full span. It seemed forever since he could just stand in the darkness and be himself. He heard someone coming up behind him and turned, watching his brother approach. Randall frowned. "I thought you were staying down home."

Marshall shrugged. "You're my little brother. I had to make sure you didn't need my help. We both know I'm the better fighter."

Randall rolled his eyes. "Thanks for your concern."

"Good evening," Liam said, appearing in the darkness. "You're feeling better?"

"Yes. Gizel's salve worked wonders." He stopped and looked at the guardians, for the first time a little apprehensive about what he had to say. "My soul mate helped too."

The guardians all nodded, looking at each other, knowing what he meant. Marshall glanced at the cabin. "Speaking of the Angel, where is she?"

"She'll be out soon."

****

The guardians came around to the front of the cabin. Karen shook her head. She couldn't believe that fairies were real and she was soul mate to a guardian of the fairy world. She couldn't wait to tell her team and her father about all this.

She hurried straight for Randall's side and sighed as he put his arm around her. She stared at the guardians towering over her. "I'm not used to being the shortest member on a team."

Marshall laughed. "You'll get used to it. Wait until you meet the rest of our clan."

"Great." She studied their faces. "What's going on?"

"We were catching up on clan business," Liam said. He stared at her. "It's time. Tell him."

Randall switched his gaze between the two of them and frowned. "Tell me what?"

"Troyington's alive," Karen said in a low voice. She felt his anger fuel his power, making it burn bright and hot within her. "He escaped after stabbing you."

"Why didn't anyone stop him?" Randall growled.

"Because saving your life was more important to all of us," she said, her voice rising. "I wasn't about to go running off to get revenge while you were leaking blood all over the ground."

He caressed her cheek. "I'm sorry."

She stared at him, trying not to smile. "Apology accepted."

Randall stared at the group. "So what do we do?"

Liam stepped forward. "He's got to answer for his crimes against my clan and Caledon's pack."

"There's no proof," Randall said. "Without that, human law can't touch him."

Karen's mouth hung open as she stared at him. "You mean he's going to get away with what he's done? Are you kidding me?"

"I didn't say that." Randall turned his gaze to the woods. "I said *human* law can't touch him. I didn't say our laws couldn't."

Karen turned to Liam. "How do we know he's still in the area? If it were me, I would've hightailed it out of here by now."

"The wood folk are watching him." Liam's face drew down into a fearsome scowl. "He hasn't left his house since he returned."

"We should be there," Marshall said.

Karen watched Liam and Marshall take off and could only imagine what a whole squadron of guardians in flight would look like. It would surely be magnificent. She turned to Randall. "Are you ready for this?"

He pulled her close. "I'm ready. The time has come to close this thing once and for all."

She checked his bandage. "It won't be too much on you, will it? I don't want you over doing it."

"Thanks to you, I'm almost completely healed. Now, hold tight to me."

She put her arms around his neck. "Like that'll be a problem."

He gathered her in his arms, stretched his wings, and took to the air.

Chapter Twenty-Two

The gargoyles landed near the trees, silently watching a figure move in the low light of the drawing room. The curtains on the french doors twitched, and the guardians faded into the shadows, becoming part of the woods that surrounded them.

Marshall turned to Randall. "How do you want to handle this, little brother?"

He flexed his fingers, staring at the house. "Wait out here."

Karen frowned, the tone of his gravelly voice making her shiver. "What are you going to do?"

"I'm going to ask him nicely to come with us." He turned to her, the look in his eyes not easing her fears. "Don't worry. The pack wouldn't forgive me if I took their revenge from them." He ripped off the bandage and silently stalked toward the house.

****

Troyington crossed to the french doors, rattling them to make sure they were locked, then headed straight for the cabinet holding the whiskey he needed for dire occasions. His hand shook as he poured a generous amount of amber liquid in a glass. The alcohol burned his throat as he tossed it back and poured another.

His men's deaths shook him more than he wanted to admit. Maybe he *had* bitten off more than he could chew on this venture. The blackness beyond concealed magical creatures who wanted his blood, and Cray and Harmon had been no challenge to them.

"How much longer before they come for me?" he asked the night.

"Not long at all," a voice rumbled behind him.

Troyington whirled around, his chest growing cold. "Dupré?" he whispered, his voice shaking. "You're alive? How'd you get in here? Everything's locked."

"I'm harder to kill than you think." Randall stepped toward him, the claws on his toes digging into the rich carpet. "For two long months, I was kept here. Did you think I wouldn't learn how to get in and out whether or not the doors were locked?"

Troyington backed away, his knees hitting the desk, his hand shaking as he held his drink. "So now what?" He took another gulp, trying to stop his voice from quavering. "You can't hand me over to the authorities. Who would believe you?" He smiled. "You must be here to kill me."

Randall narrowed his eyes. "As much as I want to, no, I'm not here to kill you."

"That's right," Troyington snorted. "As a hero and protector, murder just isn't an option for you. You can't touch me, Guardian, and you know it."

Randall grabbed the front of Troyington's shirt, lifting him off the desk. The glass fell to the floor, landing with a dull thud on the deep carpet. Randall held his hand close to Troyington's face and extended his claws. "You *will* answer for your crimes, but not to me. It's Caledon's right as pack leader to decide your fate."

Troyington's eyes widened as he finally saw

Randall's claws up close. They were longer than he thought, and he could clearly see in his mind them ripping into his flesh. He trembled harder, pushing against Randall, trying to get away. The harder he squirmed, the tighter Randall held him.

"Let me go and I'll make it worth your while," Troyington pleaded.

A deep growl rose in Randall's chest and spilled through clenched teeth as he shook Troyington as though he was no more than a rag doll.

Randall shoved him over to the french doors, the glass shattering as he kicked them open. He dragged Troyington to Liam and Marshall, dropping him at their feet. "Take him to Caledon. Karen and I will be there tomorrow."

The two gargoyles grabbed Troyington's arms, carrying him into the night sky.

****

Karen woke in bed alone with sunlight forcing her to open her eyes. She groaned and rolled over, realizing she'd been up with the sun on this entire adventure.

Randall came in and sat on the bed, his hair mussed. He grinned, making her want to throw him down right there. "It's time to go, sweetheart."

She ran a hand down his chest. "I know."

He caught her hand, lifting it to his lips. "Only a little bit more and then our time together truly begins."

She shivered with delight as goose bumps ran down her body. "Do we have a few minutes?"

His gaze traveled the length of her body under the covers. "I wish we did, but we have to get to Caledon's pack before sunset."

She gave a dramatic sigh. "All right. Let me get

dressed." She threw the covers back and stood, gathering her clothes. She felt his eyes on her and turned. "What?"

He walked around the bed and pulled her into his arms. "I'll be glad when this is over."

Her arms tightened around his waist. "I know what you mean."

He nodded, kissing her lightly. "I need to see Troyington pays for what he's done. Then, we're finished with all of this."

****

The sky faded from the light lavender of twilight to the indigo blue of night, and the moon's silver light highlighted the glow from the wall sconces. Karen stood with the two Louisiana guardians on the floor of the Great Hall as Caledon's pack gathered to give judgment on Troyington.

Karen studied the pack leader as he stood on the low stage. His eyes were hard as he stared at Troyington, but there were lines at the corners that suggested he did have another side. His brown hair was swept back from his face, the light highlighting the few silver strands. His shoulders were broad, and his chest was wide. There was no paunch around his waist, and Karen felt if he was this imposing as a man, his wolf form would probably scare the bejeezus out of people.

Karen's skin tingled as the pack leader's power rolled over her. She looked up at the rows of seats, saw every one filled, and felt the pack's anger hum in the air. Standing behind the wolves were guardians, their wings folded tight against their backs, their eyes constantly moving.

Troyington knelt before the pack leader, the heavy

chains around his wrists fed through an iron ring on the floor. His perfect hair was tangled and dirty, his clothes grimy with mud and blood. His outward appearance may have changed, but he still maintained his arrogant attitude as he glared at Caledon.

"You don't dare kill me," Troyington spat. "I'm too well known, too well connected."

Caledon's eyes glowed in the low light of the hall, and a deep growl rumbled from his chest, echoing off the walls, quieting the crowd. "Do not test me, human," he said, his booming voice echoing around the hall. "Count yourself lucky I do not gut you right here, right now."

Randall stepped forward, bowing before the pack leader. "Troyington has a point. An investigation could bring potential harm to the pack. His punishment bears careful consideration."

Caledon nodded. "Your words have merit." He glowered at Troyington. "But something must be done about him." He turned to the High Mother. "Bring your Oracle and captain to my private study. James, come with me."

Karen turned to Randall. "How long will they be?"

He watched the werewolves as they stared at Troyington, some growling deep in their throats. "As long as it takes. He asked for the Oracle. This means he's going to make his decision based on what she sees in the future."

She nodded toward the man on the floor. "Troyington's not getting out of this alive. I could *feel* Caledon's anger."

He folded his wings around her. "Caledon's furious, but he won't take a reckless course of action.

He'll do what's best for the pack. He's the best leader they've ever had."

Karen glanced in the direction Caledon had disappeared. "I can believe it."

She leaned against Randall, sighing when he held her tighter. She stared at Troyington. "I know he's done terrible things, but I can't help feeling sorry for him."

"You've got a kind heart." Randall raised her face to his. "Unlike the human world, though, fairy justice is absolute. There's no probation, no second chances. If you break our laws, you pay the price."

Karen nodded. As she stared at the gathering, she knew Troyington was doomed, no matter what Caledon decided. A door opened, and Caledon led his council back to the Great Hall. A decision had been made quicker than she would've thought.

"Randall Dupré, come forth," the pack leader commanded. Randall made his way down to stand in front of the werewolf leader. "Bradford Troyington, rise and hear your sentence."

When Troyington remained where he was, two guardians hauled him to his feet. He moved away from Randall, glaring at him.

Caledon stared at the southern guardian and Troyington. "The Oracle has seen the outcomes for the different sentences I could deliver. Guardian, I apologize for the mistreatment you suffered at the hands of this human in my service."

Randall bowed. "I would do so again to save the lives of the pack children."

"And for that, you have the eternal gratitude of the northeast pack. Every realm will know you have my favor." Murmurs filled the room, many heads nodding approval at Caledon's words.

Marshall stood behind Karen, his eyes wide. "Holy crap," he whispered.

She glanced over her shoulder at him. He looked like he was in shock. "What's wrong?" she whispered.

"No guardian has ever gotten a pack leader's favor," he replied. "Ever!"

Caledon raised his hand, quieting the assembly. "Bradford Troyington, your sentence is this. You will suffer every torment you bestowed on the Guardian, after which you will have an 'accident.' This course will draw the least amount of suspicion to my pack. Sentence to be carried out immediately."

Thunderous applause filled the chamber. Karen's knees went weak and she staggered, glancing up gratefully at Marshall when he stopped her from falling. They watched Randall make his way back to them. This was it. It was truly over. Randall swept her up in his arms, and she buried her face in his neck as Troyington was dragged from the room, screaming curses at them at the top of his lungs.

Chapter Twenty-Three

"What exactly does it mean to have Caledon's favor?" Karen asked, not sure of the entire implication.

Randall pulled her close to him. "Every being in the fairy realm knows Caledon. He's brought peace to a lot of disputes between races. He even has the respect of the vampire lords. Having his favor means that no paranormal creature in its right mind will hurt me. Basically, I now have the protection of one of the strongest packs in the world, and because you're my soul mate, it extends to you, too."

"Wow!"

"The sun will be rising soon," Marshall said. "What are your plans?"

Karen's grip tightened on Randall's arm. "I've got to go back to Troyington's estate and get my stuff. When there's an investigation into his disappearance, I don't want the police to find anything of mine in that house."

Randall looked at her for a moment. "You do realize he brought this on himself."

She nodded. "I know." She held him tight, sighing when he kissed the top of her head.

"Angel!" a small voice cried.

Karen turned just as Ari ran into her. She knelt and pulled the girl to her. "Hello, Ari. I bet you're glad to be home."

"You weren't going to leave without saying goodbye, were you?"

Karen ruffled her hair. "Of course not. I just didn't know where to find you."

"She was with me and our dad," James said. "We told him about your martial arts school, and he says he'll consider sending some of us."

"That's great, James. You can get in touch with me at the school. I'll leave the name and phone number with Liam."

James smiled and nodded. "I'll let my dad know." He grabbed Karen in a tight hug. "I hope I see you soon."

"Me, too, James," she whispered. "Me, too."

****

Randall reverted to human by the time they reached the car. He grabbed his clothes off the backseat and was quiet as they returned to the mansion. Karen kept stealing glances at him. She smiled.

Randall caught her looking and grinned. "You're a special lady, Karen."

She turned to look out the window, watching the scenery blur by. "I'll bet you say that to all the girls."

He took her hand and squeezed it. "There's only ever been you."

"Are you sure?" she asked, running her thumb over the back of his hand.

"In all my long life, I've never been surer of anything else."

Karen hesitated, then cleared her throat. "How long have you been around?"

He stared at the road. "I don't really have to answer that, do I?"

"Yes," she said, pretending to look worried. "You do."

"I'm one hundred and twenty-four."

She punched him lightly on the arm. "You're kidding, right?"

He shook his head. "I'm afraid not. I told you my race was long lived."

"So, now that I carry part of you with me, will I live that long?" She did some mental figuring.

"You should. My mother's human, and she's still alive." He slowed down, turning down the narrow drive to Troyington's driveway. She was silent as he pulled up in front of the house. He shut the car off, and they sat there. "This is something else I should've mentioned, right?"

She turned, grinning at him. "I'd say that would be a yes." She got out, gazing at him across the roof of the car. "Cradle robber."

He slowly stalked toward her, then pulled her into his arms. "Says you."

"Yeah," she murmured. "Says me."

He held her tightly for another minute, then stared at the mansion looming in front of them. "I'm going to see if Jeffries is still here."

Karen nodded and watched as he approached the front door and disappeared inside. She listened to him call for the butler, then nothing. Glancing over her shoulder, the hairs on the back of her neck stood up as a chill worked its way down her spine. She rubbed her arms, wishing Randall would hurry.

"The butler's gone," Marshall said, appearing from nowhere behind her.

Karen jumped, her heart pounding in her chest.

"You scared the life out of me. Where did you come from?" She blew out a breath. "Where's Jeffries?"

Marshall cleared his throat and looked around. "You don't really want me to answer that, do you?"

Karen thought. "No. I don't." She hesitated. "What's going to happen to this place? Who's going to let Bradford's father know?"

Marshall shook his head. "That's for the humans to do. Our part in this is over." He stopped and stared in her eyes. "Take good care of Randall for me."

"I will," Karen said. "I didn't think I'd ever find someone like him. I promise not to let anything happen to him."

Marshall smiled and nodded.

Randall came out of the house. "What're you doing here?"

"I'm on my way back to Louisiana. Just wanted to say goodbye." He grabbed Randall in a tight hug. "I'm glad you're all right, little brother. I'll see you back home."

"I should be back in a week or so." Randall thumped Marshall once on the back. "Give Mother my love. Tell the High Mother everything went as smoothly as we hoped."

Marshall nodded, squeezing Randall's arm. "See you soon. Nice to have you in the family, Karen."

"Thank you, Marshall," she said, surprised at the tender hug he gave her. "I can't wait to meet the rest of your family."

Marshall waved as he headed toward the trees. The rumble of a motorcycle filled the air, and dust floated to them as Randall's brother left the estate for good.

"He's quite the heartbreaker, isn't he?" Karen

asked.

Randall rolled his eyes. "The family just wishes he'd find his own soul mate. There are too many broken hearts in our little town."

****

Karen set the little alarm clock to wake her before the sun rose. She shivered as she yanked her clothes on and stuffed her nightshirt in her suitcase. She didn't bother turning up the heat in Troyington's mansion since it was just her, and she only had the one room. Randall would be waiting for her in the clearing at sunrise.

She carried her bags downstairs, setting them on the porch. She turned and stared at the mansion in the early light, glad to be quit of the place. The large house was eerie with just her there. She rubbed her arms, longing to get back to Angel Haven. She hurried to the back of the house, trotting to the woods to meet Randall.

She arrived just as he landed. He removed the pants he wore as the guardian and changed to his human half. He looked as glorious as he had the first morning she saw him here. The sun rose as he lifted his arms, reveling in the light that bathed him. This time, she knew how those muscles felt, how warm and smooth his skin was, the power in him. His power called out to her and she felt her own respond.

She heard the fairy music and she closed her eyes, swaying slightly in time to the ancient melodies dancing across her soul. From the look on Randall's face, she knew he was listening to the same music. She leaned her head against the tree, smiling as the music grew louder and clearer.

Randall finally turned to her, holding out his hand. She ran to him, throwing her arms around his neck, returning his passionate kisses with her own. He said nothing as he undressed her, lowering her to the ground to make love to her in the light of the new day before taking her home to Angel Haven.

****

That night, Karen took Randall to the garden her father tended to let him shift in private. His wings folded around her, and she leaned against him as they gazed at the stars.

"So, you've gotten to meet my friends. What do you think of them?"

Randall grinned. "They're an interesting bunch. They accepted me even after you told them what I am. I've never had that kind of acceptance before."

Karen nodded. "I told you not to worry. We're too varied to cast stones at others."

"You're an amazing woman, Karen." He pulled her tighter against him. "Are you sure you'll be happy with me?"

Karen turned in his arms. "Didn't you hear me tell everyone to start planning another wedding?" She poked his long, purple nose. "I told you before, no more doubts."

He rested his cheek on the top of her head and they stood in the chill night air, just enjoying holding each other.

"When do you have to return to your clan?" she finally murmured, stroking his cheek.

He closed his eyes. "I have to go back soon. I'd like to take you to meet them." He paused. "Caledon is requesting I join the northeast clan. Leaving your birth clan has only happened a few times over the centuries."

She could hear the uncertainty in his voice. She traced the scar on his chest. "Never mind anyone else. What do you want to do?"

"I'd like to stay. My clan doesn't really need me." He looked down at her. "They've got Marshall and all the others. The northeast clan had their number reduced by Troyington and his men. I'm needed here."

"Glad to hear it," she said. "Caledon sent word he wants me to teach the children martial arts."

He kissed the top of her head. "Go inside. I'll see you in the morning."

She shook her head. "I don't know if I can get used to you having to work at night. Shouldn't nighttime be ours?"

He smiled. "We'll adjust."

Karen watched him fly away and went inside. He'd be back when the day dawned. Closing the door to her room, she pulled on her nightshirt, then opened her balcony doors a crack so he could come in.

****

The floorboards creaked softly, but it was enough to pull Karen from sleep. Randall stood there, the light from the rising sun bathing him in a halo of gold.

He knelt beside the chair she had curled up in, smoothing her hair from her face. "It's dawn, sweetheart," he murmured.

She snuggled close to him as he picked her up and sighed with contentment. "Then I guess it's time to go to bed."

A word from the author...

I graduated from Mercy High in Baltimore, MD in 1981 and got married to an Air Force man in 1982. We have two amazing boys who have grown into amazing young men. We spent sixteen years in southern New Jersey, four of them at McGuire AFB. We currently live in Memphis, TN, where science fiction, wrestling, and hockey take up what time the cat doesn't.

Thank you for purchasing
this publication of The Wild Rose Press, Inc.
For other wonderful stories of romance,
please visit our on-line bookstore at
www.thewildrosepress.com.

For questions or more information
contact us at
info@thewildrosepress.com.

The Wild Rose Press, Inc.
www.thewildrosepress.com

To visit with authors of
The Wild Rose Press, Inc.
join our yahoo loop at
http://groups.yahoo.com/group/thewildrosepress/